MURDER IN WHITE

MURDER IN WHITE

A WINTERGREEN MYSTERY
BOOK 3

PATRICK KELLY

CHAPARRAL PRESS LLC

ISBN 978-1-7342392-5-6 (Print)

ONE

Early on a Friday morning in mid-January, a winter storm approached the mountain resort of Wintergreen, Virginia. Thick gray clouds covered the sky, and heavy snowfall made it difficult to see the next ridge. A fierce wind whipped through leafless forests and across frozen ski slopes. Weather forecasters predicted the storm of the decade, and few people ventured outside. For safety reasons, the resort managers took the unusual and expensive action of closing ski operations for the day.

Cassandra Key scoffed at the weather alerts on her phone. She had designated that morning for a vigorous hike in the Wintergreen forests and would not allow a bit of cold and snow to thwart her plans. After exiting her rented condo, she descended the mountain on the shoulders of two-lane roads—Blue Ridge Drive to Shamokin Springs Trail to Chestnut Place. She wore boots, black ski pants, a bright orange jacket with a hood, and gloves. The roads were quite steep in places, which required Cassandra to use her trekking poles to keep from slipping. Cassandra didn't see a single moving vehicle or pedestrian on the way. She made good time on the roads, but when she reached the access path that would take her down to Loggers Alley Trail, she slowed her pace and used the poles and careful steps to navigate the steep decline. The snow—which was now an inch thick on the road—lay in uneven clumps in the forest that disguised the way forward. Thankfully, tree blazes marked the trail.

A buzzing noise came from high above Cassandra. *What was that? Oh, no, not again, not out here on the mountain, not another blasted drone.* If there was one thing Cassandra hated most—and she hated many things—it was the sound of a drone. Progress. Consider the commercial applications, others told her. Think of the value drones would deliver to humanity. Nonsense. Cassandra frequented Wintergreen partly because of their policy prohibiting the use of drones. But on this trip, the drones were everywhere.

She could just about kill Nikki. On most tasks, Nikki performed well. She was certainly an improvement over the previous assistants Cassandra had fired. Nevertheless, Nikki should have found out that the resort had planned for a promotional drone show. The show would involve hundreds of drones, and the production company was conducting practice flights to scout the terrain. Three days earlier, Nikki stood visibly shaking in Cassandra's office and explained the situation. By then, it was too late to cancel the bookings for the club's executive retreat. Cassandra had wanted to throw something and nearly did, but the slow-count-to-five thing worked, and she dismissed Nikki with a wave of her hand.

The humming came closer, and Cassandra peered into the gray sky. The drone was bigger than most. Darn thing. Cassandra shook her gloved fist at it, and the drone scooted away. Some nerd was likely recording the storm to post it online, as if *that* would add value to the world.

At Loggers Alley Trail, Cassandra turned right. After a

short incline, the trail leveled out, and she soon reached the Outer Limits black diamond ski run. It was after ten o'clock, and under normal conditions, early skiers would be out by now, but no skiers crossed her path.

Turning to look over her shoulder, Cassandra could barely discern the ridge condos through the trees and snowfall. Bryan McCasland—that jerk—was staying somewhere in Wintergreen, perhaps in one of those buildings. Bryan served as treasurer for the Old Virginia Gun Club. He had won the position two years earlier because of his military back-office experience, and he'd been a pain in her backside ever since. Now Bryan was running a whisper campaign to unseat her as club president. Bryan outrageously claimed she was incompetent, but like all bureaucrats, he could only see the numbers. Never mind. She could take Bryan down anytime she chose. She'd dealt with more significant threats, like the old man. Cassandra shivered, but not from the cold.

Continuing on Loggers Alley Trail, Cassandra passed through a small wooded section and came onto Upper Wild Turkey run. No one skied there either, and she studied the chairlift line above her. The cables were still, and the chairs were empty. On Cassandra's previous ski trips to Wintergreen, the slopes had never been closed for the weather. Perhaps it was worse than she thought. A cloud brushed across the ski slope and obscured her view of the chairlift, but then the cloud passed, and she could see the upper lift station four hundred yards away.

Kent Olsen—the club's vice president—was staying in the Highlands complex. Cassandra recalled her evening with Kent the night before, and her hands tingled with excitement. Too bad Kent's fiancée—Elsie Dale—would arrive in Wintergreen that afternoon. Cassandra chuckled. Poor Kent. He didn't know which way to turn. His condo was on the top floor, and she could see his balcony. He might be watching for her now. Late the previous night, she had told Kent of her planned hike when she kicked him out of her condo. She squinted at Kent's balcony and thought she saw a standing figure. Cassandra waved her hands wildly to capture his attention, but then another cloud drifted across the mountain and blocked her view.

The drone she had heard earlier hovered in the clouds. The wind rushed up the mountainside and snuck inside her jacket. She had the slope to herself. Another cloud swept across the mountain, and she could hardly see fifty feet. It was like hiking in the dark. So thrilling. The wind whistled against her hood. Her hands were cold.

The Wintergreen authorities would be angry at her for hiking alone despite the storm warnings, but Cassandra couldn't help herself. She had never been a rule follower. She laughed, and the motion warmed her chest. The buzzing from another drone reached her ears, or maybe it was the same one.

What should she do with Kent? They had been reckless the previous night when they dined publicly in Staunton. He had touched her at the table and put his arm around her as they left the restaurant. Not much of a risk, because no one knew them in Staunton. Still, it struck her as unwise. He had a lot more to lose than she did. She smiled. Why should she do anything? She could predict Kent's moves. They would meet for a working lunch, and he would stumble through his decision. With his wedding growing nearer, the time had come for Cassandra and him to cease all romantic encounters. No more clandestine sleepovers. His future depended on it. She would adopt a somber expression but then agree with his suggestion. Of course, she understood. It pained her, certainly, but they would always have their memories.

And then, six months after the wedding, he would come

back to her. The risk to his future would not be mentioned. They would attend a conference together, linger over a nightcap at the bar, and wind up making out fiercely in the hallway. Then they'd be right back where they started. Now that she considered it, their affair might never end. Cassandra had no intention of committing herself to one person. She might as well keep seeing Kent off and on for the rest of their lives. Unless something unexpected happened.

But then, of course, there was Elsie Dale, the lumber heiress turned politician who had snagged Kent as her betrothed. Elsie wouldn't care to know that her husband was sneaking around with Cassandra on the side. Elsie had a lot of clout in Virginia, and she could make life unpleasant for Cassandra if she wanted to. Like all small business owners, Cassandra's financial survival depended on occupying a successful market position. Crushing Cassandra would be child's play for someone with Elsie's resources. Yes, but at the same time, Cassandra had her own kind of leverage, and if Elsie wanted to play rough, Cassandra was more than happy to oblige.

There it was again. That darn drone buzzing in the air in front of her. The cloud cleared for a moment, and she saw the drone again. Yes, it was bigger than the ones flown by middle-class drone enthusiasts. Cassandra squinted at the drone, but then the clouds rolled over her again.

The drone pulled away until it was almost out of earshot. Cassandra would take Loggers Alley Trail across the main ski area and connect with Cedar Cliffs Trail. From there, she would proceed to Pedlars Edge Trail and then take that to Blackrock Trail and the Plunge. She would push her body to the limit. It was the only way to live. Hunt. Fish. Ski. Climb. Be outdoors in nature. Close to the land. That was how she would always live her life.

The sound of a high-powered rifle firing pierced the air. A second shot followed. Cassandra scarcely felt them. The bullets forced her to take two steps backward. She experienced a sensation of falling briefly and then realized, oddly, that she was lying on the ground. The storm continued to surge against the mountain. Snow fell on Cassandra's body. Her eyes closed, and life seeped out of her onto the snow. Right at the end, with her final thought, Cassandra realized who had killed her. And why.

TWO

On the outskirts of Warrenton, Frank Richardi pulled off Route 29 into a convenience center, filled the rental car with gas, and parked in a space off to the side. Sitting in the driver's seat, Frank rubbed a hand across his face. Ugh. He was tired. He'd flown into Dulles from Martinique the previous afternoon and spent the night in a nearby nondescript hotel. Frank had not slept well. He'd risen early that morning, driven to Charlottesville for the handoff, driven even farther out to the destination, did the thing—which candidly went well—and then rode back to Charlottesville to get the rental car.

He frowned, still not sure this was a good idea. He'd promised himself and Renée that he'd never return to the states. But the client persistently reminded Frank that he had a debt to pay. He remembered the past fondly, the days when phones were attached to the wall, restaurant food was simple but tasted good, and houses were affordable. The work was easier in those days. But messy and up close and personal in a way that still interrupted Frank's sleep from time to time. There were certain images in his memory that he'd like to forget but never could. He'd told himself many times that it was a job. He delivered a service to clients who needed the service and paid well. But he'd never enjoyed the work, unlike some of the psychos he read about in novels and true crime stories. Those guys were sick. Frank did the job for a reason, and he consoled himself with the knowledge that most of the targets were slimeballs who had it coming. Yeah. Slimeballs.

Frank got out and lumbered to the convenience store. There were few other customers inside. From the checkout counter, an enthusiastic young woman with pigtails and arm tattoos called to him, "Can I help you, sir?"

"The restrooms?"

She pointed. "Over in the corner. When you get back, be sure to check out our delicious blueberry muffins. Baked this morning."

"Thank you."

When Frank returned from the men's room, he stopped at the coffee center to fix a large decaf with cream. A man in his early fifties with brown hair had already poured his coffee and reached for a plastic cover. After fastening the cover, the man turned toward Frank and hesitated. They made eye contact, and the man's eyebrows furrowed. He startled.

Frank's adrenaline cranked to the max.

Oh, jeez. I've been made.

"Harry?" said the man with a broad smile. "Is that you? Harry Worthington? It's Jim Hightower."

Frank had used different aliases in his career but never Harry. He stared at the man—Jim Hightower—trying to sort him out. Frank's mind instinctively registered the shelf of canned food three feet to his right. He could grab a can and crack this guy over the head in less than a second. Be out the door and gone in a few more seconds.

Jim Hightower leaned closer and frowned. "I'm sorry. My mistake. I thought you were a man I worked with in Philadelphia twenty years ago. It's uncanny. Your hair and nose look exactly like Harry Worthington's, but now I can see your eyes and chin are different. I apologize."

"No problem. They say everyone has a double."

Hightower shook his head and laughed. "It's uncanny. You really had me going there."

After raising a hand to signal goodbye, Hightower moseyed to the next aisle, where he joined a woman about his age. Frank took his coffee to the pastry display and selected a blueberry muffin. As the clerk ran up his transaction, Frank scanned the room. Jim Hightower and his female companion appeared to be considering snack options.

Outside, Frank retrieved his gun from his overnight bag and sat in the front seat to watch the store entrance. He sipped his coffee but ignored the muffin. Frank replayed the instant Hightower had recognized him. Was Hightower's expression that of a man who had unexpectedly come upon an old friend? Or the fearful stare of someone who had identified an old enemy? Frank chewed the inside of his mouth. After what seemed an eternity—seven or eight minutes—Jim Hightower exited the store with his companion. What had taken them so long? Without a glance in Frank's direction, Hightower and the woman got in a dark mid-size SUV and drove in the opposite direction on Route 29.

Frank heaved a sigh. Paranoia. It was not the first time he had perceived danger where none existed. Still, he'd rather be paranoid than not—his hypersensitivity to sensory input had saved his life more than once.

He slowly relaxed, and his shoulders slumped. Frank couldn't wait to get back to Martinique. Renée would pick him up at the airport, and they would stop at their favorite beach bar on the way home. Sea breezes rustled palm fronds. Jazz standards played in the background. He missed Renée's smile.

Gads, he was tired. His original plan called for him to spend the night in Manassas, but Frank changed his mind. Instead, he consulted a travel app on his phone and found a room for eighty-seven dollars at a nearby budget chain hotel. He'd take a nap and then get some food. There was plenty of time to drive to Dulles the next day.

THREE

Bill O'Shea took the last bite of a chicken salad sandwich and savored the medley of flavors—a hint of curry, grapes, and walnuts mixed with a light mayonnaise.

Cindy Quintrell sat across her dining table from Bill. She wore a long-sleeved royal-blue sweater. Her sandy blond hair, sparkling blue eyes, and shapely figure came together in a special way that Bill found immensely attractive. Cindy ran a catering business in Wintergreen and had invited Bill for lunch to thank him for helping with recent events.

"May I just say," said Bill, "that was the best chicken salad sandwich I've ever eaten."

"Thank you," said Cindy. "Although, I'm sure you said that the last time I served you chicken salad."

"Perhaps, but it's even better now. You must have tweaked the recipe."

Cindy smiled appreciatively. "Would you like some coffee and a brownie?"

"Only if you twist my arm."

Bill cleared the dishes, and Cindy fixed coffee and dessert. Cindy's two-bedroom condo was in the Vistas complex, one building away from Bill's. The single large room contained a small kitchen, a living area with a fireplace and a wall-mounted television, and a dining area with seating for six. There was scarcely room in the kitchen for Bill and Cindy to maneuver. Cindy turned, bumped into him, and laughed. A thrill passed through Bill's chest. He wanted to scoop her into his arms but was hesitant.

They were both divorced and had become an on-again, off-again couple since meeting after Bill moved to Wintergreen the prior summer. Their relationship had gone through a rough patch during the investigation of Damian Susskind's death. Afterward, Cindy wanted to remain friends but was reluctant to go further. Bill believed their romance was at an end, but then they attended the Snow Ball in December and had a marvelous time dancing. One thing led to another, and it now appeared they were on again.

Cindy leaned her hip against the counter, lifted a brownie from the plate, and took a casual bite. Bill sipped his coffee. He could watch Cindy eat brownies all day.

"Maybe we can build a fire," she said, "and watch a movie or something."

Or something? What does that mean?

"Sounds great," said Bill. "But I have to leave in ninety minutes to pick up Frieda's poodle, Curly. Frieda's leaving for a readers' convention in Florida, and I offered to keep Curly while she's gone."

Frieda Chang lived in the Cliffs complex, one building farther up the ridge. She was a successful romance writer Bill had met several months ago. Since then, Frieda had invited Bill and Cindy over for wine twice.

Cindy frowned. "She's driving down the mountain today?"

"Yes."

Cindy strode around the counter to the floor-to-ceiling windows that normally provided a stunning view of mountains cascading down to the Rockfish Valley. A low-hanging cloud drifted over the ridge.

After joining Cindy, Bill squinted to see the ski slopes below the Mountain Inn.

"The weather is better now than earlier," said Cindy, and then she pointed down and to the right. "But see there? The chairlift is not moving because they've closed the mountain today." Cindy shook her head. "Look at the clouds. See how fast they're moving? It's going to storm all afternoon and all night."

Wind whistled against the condo. Powdery snow rushed this way and that.

"Frieda should leave soon," said Cindy. "The roads will get bad in a hurry."

Much as Bill wanted to build a fire and enjoy a movie—or something—with Cindy, he felt compelled to share her warning with Frieda. He called Frieda, and at the end of a short conversation, Frieda said she was already packed and could leave in a few minutes. They arranged for Bill to come right away.

At the door to Cindy's condo, Cindy nestled close to him and hooked a finger under his belt. Their kiss lingered. Bill's hands tingled, and he wished the storm could have waited a few hours.

Then he remembered some news he had meant to share with Cindy earlier.

He said, "I forgot to tell you that my ex-wife, Wanda, is coming to Wintergreen."

Cindy's forehead creased.

"She's coming with her friend Amy," said Bill. "They've never been here or gone skiing at all, for that matter. I've told

Wanda how beautiful Wintergreen is, and she wants to check it out."

"I see." Cindy took a step back. "When is she coming?"

"Tomorrow. They'll stay three nights and then head back to Columbia."

"Is she staying with you?"

"Huh? Oh, no. They've got a two-bedroom in the Mountain Inn. I'll probably meet them for dinner or a drink. You're welcome to join us."

Cindy scrunched her nose. "Wouldn't that be awkward considering our situation? Your ex-wife and me at the same table?"

As a matter of fact, Bill thought it would be extremely awkward. He wasn't crazy about Wanda coming at all but didn't feel it was his place to tell her what to do. Bill considered Wanda a friend now and wanted to keep things that way. But the notion of a three-way conversation with Wanda, Cindy, and him made his stomach churn.

"I see your point," he said. "In case you're wondering, I didn't invite Wanda to come. It was her idea."

Cindy dropped her hands to her sides and took another step back. "It's not a big deal, Bill. Go get Curly. We can talk later."

"Yeah. Okay."

Sheesh. Whenever his relationship with Cindy began to gather momentum, something knocked them off course.

Oh, well, such is life. One step at a time.

Bill walked outside and turned left toward Frieda's condo complex. The fierce cold intruded on Bill's thoughts. He zipped his winter jacket to the top and pulled on his gloves. The wind caused the hemlocks to sway. Bare branches of deciduous trees knocked against each other. Fresh snow covered the parking lot, and Bill hurried to stay warm.

At Frieda's door, Bill knocked, and from inside, Curly barked ferociously. Frieda opened the door and smiled. Bill had to tilt his head back to make eye contact. She was one of the tallest women he had ever known. Strong too. Frieda was part Asian and had dark hair and a lovely round face. Bill often wondered whether she had played sports earlier in life, but he never raised the subject. Frieda must be tired of people asking that question.

Curly raced into the staircase landing and circled Bill's legs twice. Bill bent to rub the little white poodle behind his ears, and Curly wagged his tail.

"I'm glad you called," said Frieda. "I keep looking out the window, and the storm is getting worse by the minute."

Bill asked whether she still wanted to go. Frieda said the temperature was above freezing in Charlottesville, so she'd be fine once she was off the mountain. Frieda had already shared instructions on how to care for Curly, and they briefly reviewed them again. Her poodle was low maintenance. Walk him four or five times daily, play fetch with his ball now and again, and give him a belly scratch often. Bill could leave Curly for hours, and the dog would rest comfortably in his bed unless someone came to the door or made a noise outside the window. Then Curly barked like crazy.

"He's a great alarm system," said Frieda.

"I love a guest who earns his keep."

Frieda threw two suitcases in the trunk of her convertible, drove carefully out of the parking lot, and turned left on Blue Ridge Drive. Bill and Curly waved goodbye and slowly made their way down to the Vistas complex. The cold didn't seem to bother Curly, and he lingered to sniff at bushes yet to be covered with snow. They meandered behind the condos to observe the view. Bill's ears grew cold, and he pressed his hands against them. The Highlands Express chairlift remained still. The slopes on Blackrock Mountain and those below the Mountain Inn also appeared closed. A gust of wind blew against Bill, and he shivered.

"I don't know about you, Curly," he said, "but I'm ready to go in."

Once inside the condo, Bill settled Curly's belongings, played fetch until Curly grew tired, and then sat on the carpet next to the poodle. Curly lay on his back and nipped at Bill's hand until Bill gave him a belly scratch. What a funny dog.

Bill's phone buzzed.

It was a call from his friend Mitch Gentry, a young patrolman with the Wintergreen PD.

"What's up, Mitch?"

After the briefest of pleasantries, Mitch got to the point. A missing hiker was believed lost on one of Wintergreen's southern trails.

Bill stood and approached his picture window. An icy fog now blocked the view, and the wind howled to be let inside.

"A hiker? In this weather?"

"Yeah, it's a head-scratcher. Anyway, Fire & Rescue are marshaling resources to conduct a search. I thought maybe you could help out."

Bill froze in place. He imagined himself dressed in winter gear, standing on the side of a mountain, trying desperately to find the next trail blaze. Icy snowflakes bit his face.

"Ah, sure," he said. "I'll get my boots. I also have some extra trekking poles. Should I bring those?"

"Sorry. I didn't mean on the search team. No offense, Bill, but this will be a rough deal. We have a team of more, let's say, experienced hikers."

Bill was flooded with a sense of relief. Mitch meant they would need young, strong hikers to conduct the search. And that was fine with Bill.

"Oh. Absolutely. How can I help?"

Mitch explained that the search commander was organizing eight teams of two to begin the search. They would need drivers to ferry volunteers to and from trailheads and a couple of administrative workers to help track team positions. If Bill was willing and available, he should dress warmly and report to the fire station down the road from the Mountain Inn.

"I'll be there in twenty minutes."

FOUR

Mitch Gentry studied the Wintergreen Hiking Guide that Fire & Rescue Deputy Chief Jeffrey Tate had spread on a flat surface in the fire station. As the on-duty administrative officer, Jeffrey Tate assumed command of the search. Tate had first issued a call for young and physically fit volunteers from off-duty Fire & Rescue personnel, the resorts' operations staff, and the ski patrol. Those volunteers were gradually assembling in the fire station garage. Given the dicey weather, Tate had decreed that no one would search alone. They had enough qualified volunteers to form eight teams of two, which Tate had decided was all they could safely manage under the circumstances.

Emily Powell—Deputy Chief of the Wintergreen Police —had allowed Mitch and José Rodriguez to volunteer for the search but insisted the rest of the crew stay on duty. With the ongoing storm, the police had their hands full.

Mitch and José had done a lot of hiking in the Wintergreen area, and Tate asked them to help him organize the search tactics. The three of them now stood with a young woman named Nikki Churchill.

"What on earth possessed your boss to go hiking on a day like today?" said Tate.

Mitch thought Jeffrey could have used a more empathetic tone. Nikki Churchill stood five foot four, wore jeans and an unzipped puffer jacket, and appeared uncomfortable in the presence of three uniformed men. Her eyes flitted from Tate to Rodriguez and then to Mitch. Mitch gave her a quick smile and a nod.

Thirty minutes earlier, Nikki reported that Cassandra Key had gone hiking that morning. Nikki was supposed to pick Key up at one thirty in the small park off Blackrock Circle, but Key missed the rendezvous. Nikki had tried to reach her boss by phone without success and then waited in the park for twenty minutes before calling the police.

"She's probably fine," said Nikki. "She does this kind of stuff all the time."

"What kind of stuff?" said Tate.

"Extreme sports and that sort of thing. For example, do you know that cliff at Raven's Roost Overlook on the parkway?"

José and Mitch nodded.

"Cassandra told me that on the way up here yesterday, she stopped to climb that cliff without a rope. Twice."

Mitch frowned. He wasn't a fan of thrill seekers. They bragged of their exploits to anyone and everyone, but when they got in trouble, others had to bail them out.

Nikki Churchill had volunteered to join the search team, and Mitch admired her for doing so. But she didn't have the right clothes and had no experience hiking. When Tate informed Churchill that she didn't qualify, Churchill insisted on doing something to help. Tate said they would have some light tasks she could handle and then asked her to join them as they mapped out the search.

According to Nikki, Cassandra Key's plan had been to leave mid-morning and hike four or five miles over moderate to difficult terrain. Key had not told Nikki what route she would take, only that she would reach the lot above the Plunge at one thirty.

Jeffrey waved his hand across the lower section of the map. The map was white with light-gray contour lines and trails marked in red and yellow. "Okay, Mitch, José, which route could she take to cover five miles and end up at the Plunge?"

Mitch scrunched his eyebrows. A myriad of trails criss-crossed the land south and east of the Mountain Inn. Most of the routes included steep inclines and declines.

José pointed to the map. "There are a lot of ways to solve that puzzle. Do you see how the series of red trails makes a rough circle on the lower half of the map? If it were me, I'd go counter-clockwise, come down Wintergreen Drive to the White Oak Trail, connect to the Pond Hollow Trail, Fortunes Ridge, and then on to Brimstone and the Plunge. Alternatively, you could go clockwise by taking the access trail to hike Cedar Cliffs, Pedlars Edge, and then Blackrock Trail to the Plunge."

Mitch rubbed his chin. "That makes sense, but we also have all these yellow trails: Laurel Ridge Loop, Hemlock Springs, and the other access trails. She could have taken any one of those. Even worse, she might have lost her way and wandered off the trail. Blazes are hard to spot in this weather."

Jeffrey Tate frowned at the map. "Yeah. We can't cover everything before it gets dark, but we have enough teams to search the southeastern half of the map. If we don't find her in the first two hours, I'll call in the state."

Mitch knew the deputy chief was referring to Virginia's

Department of Emergency Management. VDEM could bring additional search teams, specialists, and more sophisticated equipment. If the search lasted into the night, VDEM might make the difference between success and failure. Then again, if the storm got any worse, it would be unwise to send teams out at all.

Tate said, "José and Mitch, we'll give each of you a partner and have you start here at the Plunge. At the bottom, split up to search the trails José outlined. We'll have other teams cover the rest of the trails."

José twisted his lips into a bunch. "If she went north, we'll miss her completely."

Tate said, "It doesn't make sense for her to go north if she planned to meet Ms. Churchill at the Plunge." He checked his watch. "And we don't have time to search the whole map."

Mitch agreed with Jeffrey's logic. In two hours, it would be almost dark. No way they could cover the whole mountain by then.

Outside, the wind howled as it blew through the forest.

Nikki Churchill's eyes remained glued to the map. She chewed her lip.

Tate asked her, "Have you tried to reach Ms. Key again?"

"I keep trying every few minutes. Still no answer."

"When was the last time you spoke with her?" Tate said, even though he had asked the same question five minutes earlier.

"Yesterday, around five thirty," said Nikki. "We worked in her condo for several hours and then she let me go."

Tate wanted to double-check the facts before sending search teams into harm's way. Nikki had sent a text to Cassandra Key that morning to warn her about the weather forecast. Her boss had sent her a curt response.

Thanks. I'll be fine.

After Nikki had called 911, Officer John Hill met her at the park, assessed the situation, and called in Fire & Rescue. Given the time constraints, Tate decided to begin the search even though the police had not yet thoroughly investigated Key's disappearance. It was theoretically possible that Key had never gone hiking at all. When Key experienced the lousy weather up close, she might have returned to her condo. But if so, why hadn't she texted Nikki about her change in plans? And why wasn't she answering her phone now? It was a loose end that needed tying off.

Tate turned to Mitch. "Someone's checking her condo, right? They'll call us if she's there."

"Yep. They're on it."

FIVE

K rista Jackson—a communications officer with the Wintergreen Police Department—fielded the call from Mitch Gentry. Mitch wanted someone to go by Cassandra Key's condo and verify that she was gone. Apparently, the person who reported Ms. Key missing hadn't seen or spoken with Key in nearly twenty-four hours.

With Mitch and José assigned to the search and the other patrol officers involved with other tasks, Deputy Chief Emily Powell asked Krista to drive by Ms. Key's condo. Krista was to pick up a key at the Mountain Inn's reception desk so she could search the unit if no one answered.

Krista got in her Subaru Forester and began the two-and-a-half-mile winding journey up Wintergreen Drive. The storm had already dropped a lot of fresh snow. No problem. The Forester's all-wheel drive had never failed her. But a fierce crosswind shook the car in the open stretches, and the snow darn near blew sideways. The heater struggled mightily, and Krista could still see her breath inside the car when she parked at the Mountain Inn. After retrieving a key from the front desk, Krista drove farther up Wintergreen Drive to the condo buildings that lined the ridge. The Overlook complex was on the right past the Vistas building where Bill O'Shea lived. Krista parked and stepped out of the Forester into what felt like a walk-in freezer. By the time she reached Key's unit, her ears were frozen. Krista never wore hats to work because she hated what they did to her hair, but why hadn't she borrowed one at the office?

At Ms. Key's unit, Krista rang the bell. No answer. Krista knocked and then knocked more loudly. Still no answer. Krista opened the door and announced herself. Then she toured the condo, turning the lights on as she went. Ms. Key was not there, but someone had definitely stayed in the unit. The coffee maker had been used but turned off. The sink contained a coffee cup, a cereal bowl, and a spoon. Two wine glasses were on a side table in the living room, one half-full of red wine and the other with a trace at the bottom. A cluster of women's beauty products lay on the bathroom counter, and drops of water clung to the sides of the shower stall. The king-size bed was unmade, and it appeared to Krista that both sides of the bed had been used, if not for sleeping, then for something else.

SIX

M itch waited with José in a squad car at the little park on Blackrock Circle. The two volunteers joining them on the first stage of the search were on the way from the fire station. Gusts of wind buffeted the car. Visibility was no more than a few hundred yards. The ground, which had begun the day with only a few patches of snow here and there, was now covered with three inches of fresh powder. Beyond the leafless trees before them was only gray. Mitch and José exchanged glances.

"Have you been down the Plunge?" asked José.

"Yes, but never in weather like this. And this is the other guys' first time."

José raised his eyebrows.

At that moment, a small SUV pulled into the lot to drop off the two volunteers. Mitch recognized Bill O'Shea's Mazda and guessed that Bill had found work as a ferry driver.

"Now or never," said Mitch, pulling on his gloves. They both wore heavy coats and boots.

Outside, they met their teammates. Mitch would hike with a young firefighter named Amari. José was paired with

Chloe, a paramedic. The four of them would descend the Plunge together. At the bottom, Mitch and Amari would hike east, and José and Chloe would take the opposite direction.

They huddled together. The icy wind stung Mitch's face. He flipped the coat's hood over his head and pulled the zipper up tight.

Amari gave the sky a worried look. "If it gets any worse, we won't be able to see our hands, let alone a hiker."

"Yeah," said Mitch. "We should have some cover on the hillside."

José led them to the trail. The first hundred feet were okay, but then they reached the Plunge. José signaled for them to come into a tight circle and then shouted to be heard above the wind.

"The Plunge is a steep rock face and will be slippery from the snow and ice, but the anchored rope will give you a solid handhold. Take it slow and keep at least one foot planted at all times. I'll go first, and Mitch will bring up the rear. Ready?"

Chloe and Amari nodded.

The Plunge dropped a hundred and fifty feet to the trail that traversed the mountainside. At the top, José took a few tentative steps on the rock surface and then crab-walked to where he could reach the anchored rope. He grabbed the rope with both hands and then straddled it with his legs. The rock face was nearly vertical. Wind gushed up from below and blew snow in all directions.

Mitch held his breath as José took another careful step and then slowly descended out of view. Chloe went next. She moved gracefully over the rock face, grabbed the rope, and lowered herself with ease. Mitch guessed that she had rock climbing experience.

Amari turned toward Mitch. His eyes looked scared.

"You okay?" said Mitch.

"Yeah. I'd rather be at the bottom, but I'll make it."

Amari moved his weight across the rock more slowly. He slipped once, and Mitch's heart skipped a beat, but then Amari grabbed the rope. With a strong upper body, Amari had no trouble descending safely from that point.

Guess it's my turn now.

Mitch figured he'd be fine since the others had managed their descents without incident. He followed their lead across the rock face to the rope and began to lower himself. Three steps down, Mitch reached an anchored eye bolt that guided the rope through a turn. He made it past the turn, lifted his right foot, and then his left foot slipped on an icy patch.

Bang.

His body slammed onto the rock, and the rope began slipping through his fingers. Mitch tightened his grip to keep from falling farther. His lungs heaved, and his legs flailed against the rock. A gust of icy air crept under his coat, and snow flew into his eyes. Even worse, his face stung like a tennis ball had struck him at high speed. With a heave, he pulled himself up enough to jam his left foot into a crevice. Once he was stable again, he paused to catch his breath.

Holy blizzard. Get me down from here.

With a laser-like focus on the task, Mitch reached the bottom without further incident.

The four searchers huddled together, and José frowned at Mitch.

"What happened? Your face is bleeding."

"It's not bad. I slipped."

As if first response was in her DNA, Chloe magically produced a white cloth and dabbed at Mitch's forehead. "It's okay," she said, but her eyes were tense. In a flash, she whipped off her backpack, pulled out a bandage, and applied it to the skin above his eye. "You'll live."

"Good thing it's this cold," said Mitch. "Otherwise, I might feel it."

In the next moment, Amari's radio crackled, and they did their first check-in with the dispatcher.

"All right," said José. "You go left. We go right. The first one to find Cassandra Key wins a round at Devils Backbone."

"You're on," said Mitch.

The two men fist-bumped to seal the bet and then parted ways.

Mitch and Amari would cover two miles on three separate trails. Their hike would descend a thousand feet and then regain much of that elevation before ending on a gravel road behind the Mountain Inn. Once there, a ferry driver would return them to the fire station for a break.

Mitch soon realized their biggest challenge was to keep from getting lost. The wind and snow made the blazes difficult to spot, and he devised a system to keep them together and on the trail. Each time they found a marker, Amari waited at that spot while Mitch forged ahead. When Mitch located the next blaze, he waved his flashlight to signal that Amari could come forward. With every quarter mile, they switched places. The system slowed their progress considerably but kept them on the trail.

Mitch's boots crunched on fresh powder. He clenched his fists to keep blood flowing to his fingers. The trail would be level for a stretch and then descend steeply. The path was rocky, and Mitch glanced down often to avoid stumbling. They saw no wildlife or footsteps in the snow from Cassandra Key or anyone else.

They reported in by radio every five minutes. After an hour, they reached the bottom of their descent and began climbing. Soon, they crossed Hemlock Springs and reached the access trail that would bring them up to the gravel road. Mitch's hands and feet grew numb, and ice formed on his eyebrows. When they finally reached the road, he was excited to see Bill O'Shea's Mazda waiting for them.

Steam poured from the tailpipes. Bill stood on the road next to the trailhead wearing a heavy coat, gloves, a black beanie, and a smile.

"You never looked so good," said Mitch.

"Hop in, guys," said Bill. "The SUV's all warmed up."

SEVEN

E arlier, Bill had reported to the fire station and volunteered to help in any way he could. A uniformed fireman asked him to wait until they had the search better organized. There was a lot of scurrying around. Other volunteers arrived, off-duty personnel from Fire & Rescue and ski patrol members. The other volunteers were younger and in better physical condition than Bill. A junior officer stopped by and asked Bill whether he felt comfortable acting as a ferry driver.

"Sure. The roads have some snow on them but very little traffic. I'll drive slowly and stick to the middle of the road."

Bill's first task was to ferry two volunteers to the Plunge to meet Mitch Gentry and José Rodriguez. Upon his return, he drove two other search teams to their jump-off points. Fitting four big adults into his Mazda was a tight squeeze, but they managed. By the time he returned to the station, no ferry work remained, and he waited for his next job.

Deputy Chief Jeffrey Tate was in charge and stood behind two seated volunteers, who were each studying a Wintergreen hiking trail map. At the end of the table, a woman—who Bill guessed was a trained dispatcher—fielded calls from search teams and then communicated with those hovering over the maps. Bill had met Jeffrey Tate, but only twice, and he was a little surprised when Tate called him by name.

"Hey, Bill. Do you know the Wintergreen hiking trails?"

"Yes. I've spent a lot of time with the map."

Tate explained what the volunteers were trying to do. They had eight search teams in the field and tracking their positions was important. Tate had instructed the teams to report in once every five minutes. He had two volunteers working to track the positions of four teams each on a large map.

Tate said, "But one of the tracking volunteers doesn't know the trails, so she's not much help." He nodded at a young woman with short brown hair. The woman leaned to her right to ask a question of the second map volunteer. Tate explained that this woman wanted desperately to help because the missing hiker was her boss. "If you could give her pointers on the map's details, she'll get the hang of it before you need to make the next ferry run."

Bill pulled up a chair, introduced himself to Nikki Churchill, and got to work. They used color-coded stickers to track each team. The search teams provided updates on distances and levels of incline, and the volunteers used the updates to move stickers along the map. In between calls from search teams, Bill gave Nikki a tutorial on the map and found she was a quick study. After twenty minutes of coaching, she didn't need his help.

The next hour passed quickly, and then Tate asked Bill to ferry a team back for a break. He made three return runs, one of which was to pick up Mitch and his search partner. Unfortunately, none of the teams reported any signs of a hiker. Back at the station, Tate and Mitch and José huddled over the map and outlined more search missions to conduct. After a quick break, Bill ferried two search teams out again. On his return drive, he fretted over the coming darkness. By then, they had covered most of the southern trails, and the storm showed no signs of letting up.

Apparently, Tate also had concerns because when Bill reached the fire station, he discovered that Virginia's Department of Emergency Management had arrived. Deputy Chief Tate pulled him to one side.

"Thanks, Bill. I appreciate your help, but I've passed the command over to VDEM. They have resources and their own methods, so we won't need you any longer."

"Sure. Glad to lend a hand."

Tate walked away, and Bill lingered to absorb the sight of VDEM swinging into action. Then Nikki Churchill approached him.

"Thanks for helping me with the map."

"You bet."

"I'm surprised they haven't found her yet. But I'm sure they will. Don't you think so?"

"Ah, let's wait and see." Although an optimist generally, Bill didn't feel confident the rescue attempt would result in a happy ending.

"Is there anything else I can do?" asked Nikki.

Then Bill's cell phone buzzed. It was Cindy. He held a finger up toward Nikki in a silent request for her to give him a moment. Bill answered the call and learned that Cindy—who felt compelled to do something to assist the search—had spent the last several hours making a big batch of chili, a large salad, cornbread, and several dozen brownies. Did Bill think the volunteers would want some chili? Yes, he did. After the call, he asked Nikki if she would help him fetch the food.

On the drive up from the fire station, dark gray clouds hovered above them, but a lull in the storm quieted the wind. Nikki seemed a little nervous, so Bill tried using conversation to distract her.

"How long have you known Ms. Key?" he asked.

Nikki had worked as Cassandra's personal assistant for three years. Cassandra owned a small chain of gun stores in a Southeastern Virginia area that included Norfolk, Virginia Beach, and Chesapeake. Cassandra earned her income from the retail business, but her passion was the Old Virginia Gun Club, a social organization over which she had presided for the last four years.

Bill's tactic of distracting Nikki with easy questions seemed to calm her, so he continued.

"I've never heard of the Old Virginia Gun Club. Tell me about it."

The name conjured in Bill's mind a highbrow society formed by white men in wigs during the colonial era, but apparently, it had only existed since the 1950s. The founders believed adding the word *old* to their new organization's name would lend it class, a tactic that worked, because they soon attracted a large group of hunting enthusiasts who also had money. The club organized local hunting excursions for deer and duck and long-distance trips for more exotic game— moose and elk in North America and the big five in Africa.

"I see," said Bill. Though Bill had never hunted wild animals for food or sport, he knew plenty of others who did. "What about you, Nikki? Are you into guns and hunting?"

"No, I'm here for the job. I've never been hunting at all. It's weird, I guess, working for a gun lover, but Cassandra pays well, and she certainly keeps me busy."

Nikki seemed happy to share her knowledge of the Old Virginia Gun Club. Cassandra Key's grandfather had been one of the club's founding members, and her family remained enthusiastic supporters. But hunting among the wealthy had experienced a decline in popularity over the years, and the gun club's membership had fallen. Since taking the reins as president, Cassandra had worked like a demon to stimulate interest in the club without success. It was somewhat ironic, Nikki thought, that even while Cassandra's retail gun sales beat projections every year, the gun club grew steadily less relevant. Determined to devise a strategy to reverse the decline, Cassandra had organized a winter retreat for the club's executive trustees.

"And by retreat," said Bill, "you mean a combination of work and play here in Wintergreen?"

"Exactly," said Nikki.

"Why would Cassandra hike alone if other board members are here?"

"Honestly, Cassandra is a loner." Then, as if fearful that she had spoken out of turn, Nikki hastened to add, "I mean, she's good with people when it comes to business, but she goes her own way on her time."

"She's not married?"

"Uh, no."

By the tone of Nikki's voice, Bill gathered the young woman was sure her boss would never marry. He glanced at Nikki's face and guessed she was in her early thirties. With an olive complexion and dark hair that she wore short, Nikki might have been Latina. He then recalled a question that had popped into his mind when he first heard Nikki's full name.

"You're the first Churchill I've ever met," he said. "I have to ask. Any relation?"

Nikki laughed.

"Sorry," said Bill. "You probably get that all the time."

"No problem. No relation that I know of. My grandfather was English and moved to the US in the 1950s, but my mother is from Mexico. If we dug deep into our genealogy, we might find a connection to Winston Churchill's ancestors, but no one has ever cared to do the work."

Bill smiled. Every American had a different story. His Irish roots traced to Philadelphia in the mid-twentieth century and to Ireland fifty years earlier. He had done some research using a genealogy site and learned his family came from County Cork. Maybe someday he'd go over there and tour the country for a week or two. Might be fun.

Bill parked at Cindy's building and led Nikki inside. At the door, Cindy gave Bill a quick hug and grabbed his hands.

"Gosh, I'm so worried about this missing hiker," she said. "Do you think they'll find her?"

"Ah, Cindy, this is Nikki Churchill. She volunteered to help me carry the food."

"I'm sorry," said Cindy. "I'm being so rude. Please, come in."

Bill hastened to share that Nikki was the missing hiker's assistant. Cindy's eyes widened when she understood Nikki's personal connection to the emergency, but Nikki didn't seem fazed.

"Don't worry," said Nikki. "I'm sure they'll find her. They have like this huge team now. And Cassandra can take care of herself. No doubt."

Nikki turned toward the counter where the food was organized, and Cindy exchanged a worried look with Bill. Unlike Nikki, Cindy apparently shared Bill's view that Cassandra Key was in grave danger. Darkness was closing in, the temperature was dropping, and the storm could surge again at any moment. Nikki suffered from the irrepressible optimism of youth, and Bill guessed that she had little to no experience with death. He hoped this wouldn't be her first.

The storm worsened on Bill and Nikki's return drive to the fire station. Another inch of snow covered the road. What a storm. Why would anyone venture out in this mess? Nikki had described her boss as an aggressive sports enthusiast and a loner.

And maybe a little crazy too.

Bill would be glad to drop off the food and return to care for Curly. At the station, there were so many vehicles that Bill had to squeeze the Mazda into an awkward space. At the back of the SUV, he loaded Nikki's arms with the covered salad and a big container of brownies. He grabbed the pot of chili, left the cornbread for a second trip, and turned to follow Nikki inside.

Suddenly, Nikki's left foot slipped on ice, and she twisted her body to keep from dropping the food.

Bill's eyes grew wide.

Nikki fell, her arm whacked against the pavement, and she cried out in pain.

Bill hurried to her side, placed the chili on the ground, and crouched next to her. Her face was strained. Miraculously, the salad and brownie containers had landed without spilling their contents.

"Are you okay?" he said.

Nikki clutched her right forearm. "No, I don't think so. I may have broken my arm. It hurts like hell."

"Oh, no. Jeez. No, don't try to stand. Sit here, and I'll get help."

"At least I didn't spill the salad."

But the injury hurt too much for Nikki to laugh at her own joke.

EIGHT

The WinTergreen search teams returned to the command post with nothing to report, and then VDEM assumed command of the search. A Wintergreen paramedic examined Nikki's forearm and concluded that the fall fractured her ulna and radius bones. The breaks had not pierced the skin, which was good news; nevertheless, an EMS team took Nikki to the Augusta Medical Center for additional treatment. Bill had no role in that, so he returned home to care for Curly, eat some dinner, and build a fire.

Later, Bill poked at the fire and studied the flames. Curly got up from his bed and nestled close to Bill's ankle for attention. Bill scratched behind Curly's ears, and the poodle lay on his back for a belly rub. While he rubbed Curly, Bill fretted over Cassandra Key being out in the storm.

The storm had surged again and brought high winds that moaned as they swept through the trees. Bill poured another splash of red wine into his glass and stepped to the picture window. He couldn't see a thing. Curiosity soon got the better of him, and he donned his winter coat and ventured onto the balcony. The snow blew sideways and struck Bill's cheek.

Thick clouds covered Wintergreen, and he couldn't see the ski slopes. On the right, he glimpsed light coming from Cindy's building.

A gust rocked Bill on his feet, and he shook his head. How could anyone survive such a night in the open? Animals hid in burrows and caves and the rotted hollows of dead trees. He imagined himself in the forest, stumbling in the dark, searching for a low spot where he could nestle in and pull branches and leaves over his body. What a nightmare.

Bill walked inside and locked the door, glad to be warm and dry.

NINE

Lewis Hancock stood at the top of the Wild Turkey ski run and carefully searched the hillside below him. It was seven fifteen in the morning. The raging storm had hampered VDEM's efforts overnight, but the weather cleared enough by seven for them to commence the search in earnest. As a start, VDEM asked the ski patrol to do a thorough sweep of every run.

In truth, no one expected to find Ms. Key on a ski run, but they could cover the ground quickly and at little cost. So, the ski patrol captain assigned Lewis and three others to search the Highlands Express area.

The temperature was in the low teens. Lewis was the oldest ski patrol member, had skied at Wintergreen for over four decades, and knew everything there was to know about safety on the mountain. But despite having all the proper clothing, he could feel the cold seeping into his bones. Lewis couldn't imagine a hiker surviving the night out in the open.

The other patrol members lacked patience. One of them skied ahead of Lewis on the Wild Turkey ski run. The younger skier carved sharp turns down the mountain and covered a lot of ground quickly, probably figuring that would improve his chance of spotting a lost hiker on the hillside. But the storm had dumped eight to ten inches of fresh powder, and Lewis knew that a person lying in a low spot could be covered in white by now, so he took his time. He skied to one side of the hill, inspected the woods beyond the run, then skied to the other side and repeated the process. A skier suffering from hypothermia could stumble under the trees to rest and become too weak to call for help.

It took Lewis fifteen minutes to reach the bottom of the hill, but despite his care, he found nothing out of place on the Wild Turkey ski run. He rode the Highlands Express chairlift to the top and decided to search the run a second time. He might have missed something. Snow had drifted against chairlift support towers and formed fresh moguls in other places.

Using long slow sweeps across the run, Lewis tried to search different ground than he had on his first trip. A third of the way down, Lewis approached the area where Loggers Alley Trail crossed the hillside. Boot prints indicated that at least one search team had already come that way. Lewis squinted and then skidded to a stop beneath an oddly-shaped fresh mound of snow under the chairlift cable. What was that? A black spot in the snow not much bigger than a quarter. Lewis side-stepped his skis back up the hill and bent toward the snow, still unable to identify the object. He reached to brush the snow away and realized the black spot was from a boot. His heart thumped wildly.

Lewis fell to his knees and tore at the snow with his gloved hands. He managed to free enough of the boot to know it was attached to a leg. After popping off his skis, he used one to jab at the snow, hoping he was wrong. When the cleared snow revealed a flash of orange, Lewis gasped. He brushed more snow away from the jacket until he found a sleeve and Cassandra's Key's wrist. Lewis knew what he would find, but he had to check for a pulse anyway. Key's wrist was ice cold.

Lewis's shoulders sank. He knew how to handle many a crisis on the mountain, but he could only call it in this time. Lewis's role had come to an end.

TEN

Hours later, Frank Richardi awoke, showered, and walked outside to inspect the hotel parking lot. He counted the vehicles—seventeen, primarily SUVs and sedans, two pickups, and one van with a logo on the side for a plumbing supply business. Frank assessed the distribution of guests as typical for a small hotel on the outskirts of a small city. While Frank watched, a man exited the hotel with a roller bag, loaded it in the trunk of his Camry, and drove off.

The hotel provided a continental breakfast for free, but Frank had a long day ahead and craved a more substantial meal. The morning was brisk, but it was only a few blocks to the pancake house he had noticed the previous night. He cut through the parking lot of a restaurant to one of the main roadways that ran through town. From there, Frank took the sidewalk past a paint and body shop, an auto repair shop, and a local bank to arrive at the pancake house. The restaurant was half full. The hostess offered him a table in the middle of the room, but Frank asked for a booth next to the window where he could keep an eye on the parking lot and the front door.

The food in Martinique was good, but he missed certain meals unavailable on the island. Some mornings, nothing beat a steaming stack of buttermilk pancakes with a side of bacon and good old-fashioned syrup. His jacket lay on the bench seat next to him, his pistol within easy reach. The incident with the stranger in the convenience store had unnerved Frank, but he'd noticed nothing out of order in the intervening time. Still, he kept a careful watch on his surroundings. There were three families in the dining room, plus four couples and several men eating alone. None of the men paid him the slightest attention. They focused on their food or their phones. One older guy read a newspaper.

On the road outside the window, morning traffic picked up—construction vehicles, delivery trucks, people going to work. The waitress brought Frank's breakfast and then freshened his coffee. As he ate, Frank considered his schedule for the day. His Dulles flight didn't leave until three thirty, which allowed time for him to do some light shopping for Renée. Certain items were expensive in Martinique, and Renée often went without. Frank had asked her to make a list—he was confident a northern Virginia mall would have everything.

Frank had never been a happy man until he met Renée. He had grown up in an angry household and without much money. The only positive trait he'd known for most of his adult life was loyalty. Loyalty to bad people. But then he had retired to Martinique with a new identity and met Renée. She introduced him to kindness and joie de vivre. Their attraction was based on chemistry at first but soon grew into much more. He had shared with Renée that his past was ugly and that she shouldn't want to know any more about it than that. Renée had been willing to judge him based solely on how he lived his life in Martinique. He had a new life, and everything was great for several years.

Then, he received an email from an anonymous source that turned out to be the client. The client played the loyalty card. Certain people had provided the necessary permissions that allowed Frank to retire, and Frank owed a debt to those people. He could have ignored that debt and probably never had to pay a penalty. But in the end, loyalty won.

The client made a specific request. They wanted a job done with no risk of blame being laid at their door, and they were prepared to wait for as long as it took. So, Frank had done his homework and put together a zero-risk plan. It took time for the various parts of Frank's plan to come together in the right way. Three days ago, Frank concluded that everything was in place, and he packed a bag. That night, he promised Renée this would be his last trip to the US. And he would never break that promise.

After breakfast, Frank stopped in the restroom and then stepped through the pancake house's front door. He inhaled the crisp, clear air and then sensed an uneasy tingle across the back of his shoulders. Frank faced straight ahead, but his eyes carefully scanned the far edges of his peripheral vision. A young woman in casual attire carried a clipboard into the garage of the auto repair shop. A dark blue compact drove through the bank's ATM lane. Across the street, customers pumped gas at a Sunoco. Frank noticed nothing out of place. Still, he cut through the back of the parking lot to a residential street with no sidewalk, then used that street to return to his hotel. There was no traffic.

Try as he might, Frank couldn't shake the feeling that someone was watching him.

ELEVEN

After a restless night's sleep, Bill arose to find Curly growling next to the drapes at the back window.

"What's the matter, boy? Need to go out?"

Curly barked.

"Okay. Okay."

Bill pulled the drapes to the side. Gray clouds covered the sky, but the storm had lifted. The trees were still, and the mountains across the hollow were visible once more.

Curly lifted his front legs to the windowsill for a better view. He barked again.

"All right. All right. Give me a second, will you?"

Outside, a thick blanket of fresh snow covered the ground and brushed against Curly's belly. But that didn't slow Curly down. He was mightily agitated and yanked on his leash to lead Bill behind the building to where the lawn ended and the hillside fell away. Snow covered the mountains as far as Bill could see. A hint of fireplace smoke lingered in the air. The temperature remained below freezing, and Bill zipped his coat to the top.

Curly growled low in his throat and yanked on his leash

as if he wished to run down the steep slope. What had gotten into him? Movement on the other side of a stand of leafless trees caught Bill's eye.

A cluster of people gathered on a ski run underneath the Highlands Express chairlift. Several police vehicles with flashing lights were parked on the snow-covered dirt road that ran laterally across the mountain. His eyes followed the ski run from the vehicles up to the lift station. A heavy weight settled on Bill's chest because he knew the presence of law enforcement personnel must be related to the missing Cassandra Key.

His cell phone buzzed in his pocket. It was Emily Powell, deputy chief of Wintergreen's police department.

"Hey, Emily," he said.

"Morning, Bill. Sorry to bother you so early. We have a situation."

"Yeah. I might be looking at it right now. I'm walking a friend's dog and can see some of your team under the Highlands Express chairlift."

"Uh-huh. We found Cassandra Key. I'm afraid she's deceased."

Bill took a deep breath and blew the air out slowly. Ms. Key was in her late thirties, far too young for such a fate.

"Do you know what happened?" he said.

"It's unclear at this point. The body was covered in snow. Apparently, no one noticed her on the hill due to the low-hanging clouds we had yesterday."

Emily explained that state forensics were on the scene, and the ME was driving in from Roanoke. In addition, she had spoken with Undersheriff Arnie Shields at the Nelson County Sheriff's Office.

"Here's the thing, Bill," Emily said, "with Alex on vacation in Florida and two open positions, I'm a bit strapped. I wonder if you could help me out."

Police departments across the country struggled to fill open positions created by record-high resignations and retirements. Wintergreen had lost its chief and lead investigator in the last six months, which led Alex Sharp, a long-term Wintergreen resident and real estate broker, to step in as acting chief. Knowing that Bill was a retired homicide detective, Alex had asked for Bill's assistance several times. Now, Emily was doing the same thing.

"Of course," said Bill, "if you believe I can be of assistance."

"I do. I mentioned the idea to Arnie, and he agrees that having another experienced mind on this would be a big help."

Bill studied the clump of people gathered under the Highlands Express chairlift where Ms. Key's body had been discovered. The people were clearly distinguishable from the white snow and the dark, leafless trees. Surely, someone had seen Cassandra Key lying there yesterday. Then Bill recalled that he and Curly had stood in the same place after Frieda Chang left for her trip, and Bill hadn't seen a body lying on the ski run. The storm had ebbed and flowed from the time it hit the mountain. At times, the snow was falling so hard it would have covered a body in less than an hour.

"Um," said Emily. "One other thing I should tell you."

"What's that?"

"There's apparently a lot of blood at the scene."

Bill frowned. "Blood?"

"Yeah, the ski patroller who found Ms. Key believes she was shot."

TWELVE

"She was shot twice in the chest by a high-powered rifle," said Soren Larsen.

Soren Larsen was the state medical examiner for the central region of Virginia, headquartered in Roanoke. He had squeezed his bulky middle into a chair at one end of the table in the Wintergreen police station's single conference room. Undersheriff Arnie Shields from Nelson County and Deputy Chief Emily Powell from Wintergreen joined Larsen at the table, as did Bill. Mitch Gentry stood near the whiteboard mounted on the wall.

By the time Soren drove from Roanoke to Wintergreen and performed his initial examination of the body, the morning had grown late, so Emily arranged for two large pizzas to be brought into the meeting. After delivering his attention-grabbing opening statement, Soren reached for a second slice.

"A high-powered rifle?" said Arnie Shields. His eyes bugged open. "On a ski slope? In the middle of a storm?"

"That's what I said."

Soren had a flair for the dramatic, which is why he had

teased them with a one-line opener. Bill paid him no mind; he knew Soren would give them what they wanted sooner or later. Emily was junior to Arnie, both in terms of jurisdiction and experience. She kept her face neutral.

"Okay," said Arnie. "Let's hear the details."

Larsen continued. "I believe one of the bullets pierced her heart, which caused her to bleed to death quickly."

"What sort of caliber?" said Arnie.

"I don't know and won't know for sure unless we recover one or both rounds, which may never happen. However, I know the bullets entered her chest, traveled through her body, and left relatively small exit wounds. That suggests a large-caliber cartridge fired by a high-powered rifle, the sort of weapon a big game hunter might use."

Good lord, thought Bill, *a hunting rifle? Here in Wintergreen?*

The room grew quiet as the law enforcement officers absorbed the ME's revelations. Emily Powell pulled her shoulders back. Mitch Gentry chewed on his lip.

Finally, Arnie asked, "Can you estimate the time of death?"

"All I can say at this point is her body lay in single-digit temperatures all night. I'll need the autopsy to get you a better estimate."

Emily said, "What else can you tell us?"

Soren pulled his chin. "From the body's position, I could discern that she was facing the top of the slope when she was shot. If she was hiking laterally across the hill, she must have stopped, turned to face uphill, and then been shot."

"Do we know what she was doing there in the middle of a snowstorm?" asked Arnie.

"We have a good guess," said Mitch.

At Emily's request, Mitch had taped an enlarged hiking

trail map to the whiteboard. Standing at the map, Mitch brought Arnie and Soren up to speed on the previous day's events, including Ms. Key's missed rendezvous at the Plunge and the subsequent search efforts for her on the southern trails. Mitch pointed at the trail map.

"We now believe Ms. Key began her hike somewhere in the northern section." Mitch pointed at the trail map. "She could have taken the access trail from Chestnut Place down to Loggers Alley Trail and then turned south." Mitch marked an X on the map. "She was found here. It's also possible she started at other points on the map, although those would have required a longer hike from her condo on Blue Ridge Drive."

Arnie nodded thoughtfully and then said, "Someone should have heard the rifle shots."

Emily told Arnie they had yet to ask residents for leads. Given the high winds, it was possible that no one had noticed the shots above the storm.

Bill had a follow-up question for the medical examiner. "Can you tell us where the killer was standing when they pulled the trigger?"

Soren played with his ear. "Probably not. I'll be able to determine the angle of entry. With that information, you might be able to logically determine possible vantage points for the killer."

"That could be helpful," said Bill.

With no more questions to answer, Soren promised to report back when he had more information and then left.

Arnie and Emily discussed the next steps. As Nelson County had a lot of other territory to protect, Arnie would assume an oversight role and have regular calls with Emily to coordinate interdepartmental efforts. Emily would assign Krista Jackson full-time to the investigation. Krista would send a blast communication asking Wintergreen residents to report anything unusual they had noticed in the Highlands area the previous day. For now, they would keep secret the news that Ms. Key had been murdered by saying their request for information was related to the reported missing hiker. Krista would field incoming calls and emails and sort valuable leads from the rest.

Mitch was also assigned full-time to the investigation. He and Bill would work as a team to interview anyone who knew Ms. Key and had been in Wintergreen at the time of her death.

They would start with Nikki Churchill.

THIRTEEN

M itch and Bill passed two snow plows on the way up the mountain from the police station. Bill's drive down that morning had been a white-knuckle affair, but with Mitch behind the wheel of the squad car and patches of dark pavement showing through the snow and ice, Bill now managed to relax in the passenger seat.

Mitch parked in the registration lot for the Mountain Inn. Nikki Churchill was staying in a studio room in the main building, and they hoped to find her there. They had her phone number, but Bill preferred to deliver the news face to face.

On their way from the car to the inn's entrance, they encountered a drone hovering twenty feet above the parking lot. Both men stopped to observe the flying object. Given Wintergreen's policy prohibiting the use of drones, they were a rare sight at the resort until the arrival of the drone show production company.

Was the hovering machine filming Bill and Mitch, and if so, to what end? At that moment, it occurred to Bill that drones might have been a great help on the search for

Cassandra Key the previous day. Though unfamiliar with the subject, Bill guessed there were many commercial drone applications. Nevertheless, he yearned for the peace and quiet that would return after the show.

At Nikki's door, they stood side by side, and Mitch knocked. Footsteps approached from inside, and the door opened. Nikki wore a short-sleeved shirt with a jean jacket draped over her shoulders. Her right arm was in a cast and sling, and her face brightened when she recognized Bill.

"Did you find Cassandra?" she asked.

Bill cleared his throat. "I'm afraid we have bad news."

Nikki's face grew dark as if Bill's words had confirmed her worst nightmare. "She's dead, isn't she?"

"Yes."

Nikki left the door open and turned to go sit on the couch. The studio was small, with scarcely enough room for the queen-size bed, sofa, television, and tiny kitchen. Bill and Mitch followed Nikki into the room.

Bill had worried about Cassandra when he stood on his balcony the night before. He had doubted anyone could survive being outside in such a storm. Nikki must have had the same concerns, but she didn't have the whole story yet.

When Bill explained that they had found Cassandra shot dead on a ski slope, Nikki gasped, and her left hand flew to cover her mouth. Bill told Nikki that this changed things. The search for a missing hiker had now become a murder investigation.

"Murder!" she exclaimed. The muscles in Nikki's arms and shoulders grew stiff, and her eyes darted from Bill to Mitch. "Someone murdered Cassandra? Oh, this is awful." Nikki's hand fell to her lap, her shoulders hunched, and she began rocking slowly.

Bill feared that Nikki would soon openly cry. He sat

beside her and signaled for Mitch to sit in a nearby chair. Bill was prepared to give Nikki as much time as she needed. He knew from experience that people processed this sort of news in different ways. Family members often broke down completely, but from his previous conversation with Nikki, Bill understood that her relationship with Cassandra was strictly professional. Still, when Nikki sniffed, he jumped up to fetch a box of tissues from the kitchen counter. He let another full minute pass, which was a long time for people to sit together in silence.

"Nikki," he finally said, "we need to ask you some questions when you're ready. We need your help with the investigation."

Sometimes people needed a prompt to spur them out of shock. This time, it worked.

Nikki blew her nose, straightened her shoulders, and gave Bill a short nod. "Of course, whatever you need."

"Yesterday, you told me Ms. Key was here in Wintergreen for an executive retreat of some sort. Can you tell us more about that? Specifically, we want to know who is here and their relationships with Cassandra."

Once she got started, Nikki delivered information efficiently. The Old Virginia Gun Club executive board included four members: Cassandra as president, the vice president Kent Olsen, the treasurer Bryan McCasland, and the trustee emeritus Allen Steele. Kent Olsen and Bryan McCasland had arrived at Wintergreen two days earlier, as did Cassandra. Allen Steele was quite old and would not attend the retreat.

"Is anyone else coming?" said Bill. "Spouses? Partners?"

Nikki nodded. "Elsie Dale. She and Kent Olsen are engaged to be married. I believe Ms. Dale was scheduled to arrive sometime yesterday, but you'll have to confirm that with Kent."

Mitch leaned forward. "She's not *the* Elsie Dale. Is she?"

"Uh-huh."

Bill frowned. He was unaware of that name. Perhaps Dale was an entertainment celebrity or a social media influencer. He paid little attention to those worlds. "Who's Elsie Dale?"

"She's a representative in the Virginia House of Delegates," said Mitch. "Lulu follows state politics and keeps me informed. Elsie Dale defeated Beau Adams—a multi-term Republican incumbent in the Chesapeake district—by running on a climate-change campaign. Adams is a climate-change denier, and the campaign got a lot of attention. It was big news here in Virginia but probably didn't warrant coverage down in Columbia."

"I see," said Bill.

"But that's not all," said Nikki. "Elsie Dale is also the sole heiress to the family fortune. You know, the Dale Corporation?"

"The lumber company?" said Bill.

"That's right," said Nikki. "But the Dale Corporation has expanded far beyond lumber. They're into brown-paper packaging and recycled consumer products. It's a multi-billion-dollar business and still privately owned. Of course, that's how Elsie funded her campaign."

"Would anyone else have known Cassandra was here in Wintergreen?" asked Bill.

Nikki shook her head. "Not that I know of. Of course, she might have told any number of people, but I doubt it. Cassandra didn't advertise her schedule to others, and she didn't have a lot of friends."

"What about the retail business?" asked Bill.

"She has a good management team in place. They generally go through me for routine stuff. They know how to contact Cassandra directly if they need her, but they rarely do."

Bill shifted his weight on the couch. The interview would become trickier as they went along.

"We believe the killer shot Ms. Key with a rifle," he said. "Would you know whether any of the people we've discussed is proficient with a rifle?"

Nikki's eyes moved from Bill to Mitch. Her expression suggested they were not too bright.

"All of them," she said. "They're all proficient with rifles. They hunt big game for fun. I suppose Elsie Dale doesn't fall into that category, but even she has been learning the sport. Kent Olsen takes her on trips. She might believe hunting credibility will enhance her political prospects."

"She may be right," said Bill.

"And you, Nikki?" said Mitch. "Are you proficient with a rifle?"

"Me? Oh, no." Nikki turned her head toward Bill. "Like I told you yesterday, I've never even fired a gun. Of course, working for Cassandra for the last three years, I've learned something about them. Cassandra offered to pay for me to have lessons, but it's not my thing."

"Makes sense," said Bill, to kill time. It appeared they had a narrow range of suspects and might be able to conclude the investigation quickly. But he could use a little more help from Nikki. So far, he had sought factual information. Now, he wanted her opinion.

"Can you think of a reason why any of the persons we've discussed, or anyone else for that matter, would want to harm Ms. Key?"

Wrinkles formed on Nikki's forehead. "No. Kill her? No. Candidly, Cassandra wasn't the easiest person to get along with. She had arguments with everybody, and occasionally, the arguments grew heated, but I can't imagine anyone wanting to cause her physical harm."

"Are there any specific arguments that stand out in your mind?" said Bill. "Not necessarily a disagreement from the last week or two. It might be something that happened a long time ago."

Nikki lifted her left hand to rub her eye.

Mitch pulled his phone out of his pocket, tapped a few buttons, and studied the screen.

"I thought of something," said Nikki. "It probably doesn't mean anything. When I began working for Cassandra, she was in a relationship with Kent Olsen, the club's vice president. It wasn't well known. Cassandra liked to keep her private affairs private, but they saw a lot of each other. I expected them to get married, but Cassandra suddenly broke it off."

Bill said, "What was Mr. Olsen's reaction to Ms. Key's decision?"

Nikki lifted her shoulders nonchalantly. "He seemed fine. His interactions with Cassandra and me were professional and cordial. I didn't detect any tension between them, but people are hard to read sometimes. Anyway, Kent is now engaged to marry Ms. Dale, so I guess he's fine."

Mitch cleared his throat to get Nikki's attention. "One of my colleagues visited Ms. Key's condo yesterday when we were conducting the search. The officer said a guest had been with Ms. Key the previous night. Do you have any idea who that might have been?"

Nikki frowned. "No. Two nights ago? She didn't have an engagement on her calendar. She told me she was having takeout and would make it an early night."

"Okay," said Mitch. "Thanks."

"Can you think of anything else that might help us?" said Bill.

Nikki had nothing else. Bill encouraged her to get in touch if anything else came to mind. Then he asked her for the other board members' contact information. Nikki forwarded the information from her phone to Bill, but her eyes were troubled. She seemed disturbed.

"What's the matter?" said Bill. "Do you want to meet with someone? A grief counselor?"

"It's not that," Nikki said. "I don't know what to do. Should I tell the retail managers? Also, Kent will want to make a statement to club members. Is that okay? I don't even know if I have a job. I guess I don't, actually, because Cassandra employed me personally."

Nikki's mind spun in the vacuum created by the sudden loss of Cassandra Key.

Bill put a hand on her good arm. "Listen, don't do any of that stuff now. Go to the lobby, get a warm drink, and read a book if you can. Someone from the Wintergreen police will be in touch. We may need your help contacting family and so forth."

Nikki breathed deeply and then nodded.

"It'll be okay," said Bill. "I promise."

FOURTEEN

"Here, try this one, Frank," the sales associate said. "It has hints of amber and musk. Sexy, but not in your face. It's subtle. Seductive."

Frank took the offered tab and lifted it to his nose. Hmm. She was right. That *was* seductive.

With plenty of time to spare, Frank had spent ten minutes at the Tous les Jours fragrance counter. The associate reminded him of his mother—medium height, a birdlike figure, and friendly. The associate had asked Frank to describe the gift's intended recipient and offered him perfumes to sample. He expressed interest in three, which she placed to the side. Now, they revisited those three. It was difficult to decide, and he asked the associate for her opinion. "Is this for a lover?" she asked. His expression must have given him away because she didn't wait for a verbal answer. "You must go with Night after Night." With that decision made, Frank asked for the larger bottle, and the associate rang up the purchase.

Frank had found everything on Renée's list, even the brand-name exercise outfit that she swore was never available online in her size. He had half a dozen shopping bags that now cluttered the floor around his feet. The associate rang up his purchase, and Frank carefully inserted two smaller bags inside larger bags. The perfume was not on Renée's list. He had learned over time that whenever he bought her presents, the surprise gifts inevitably delighted her the most. The Night after Night fragrance would earn him a big kiss.

Frank's unease had left him that morning as soon as he got in the rental car and left the parking lot. He was headed home and would see Renée that night. It was natural for him to be on edge after an assignment, but no one cared about an old operator like him. Who would even remember him? He had done nothing of note in the last five years. To suspect he was on anyone's radar at this point was egotistical. He felt like whistling, a talent he had honed as a boy but suppressed when it became essential to travel unnoticed. In Martinique, he had rediscovered the joy of listening to his own music. He didn't know where the tunes came from half the time. But Frank pressed his lips tightly together. He wasn't home yet.

Carrying the packages, he exited Tous les Jours and turned left on the second-story walkway of the mall. The mall was an open atrium with three levels, and it would take him ten minutes to reach the garage. Frank kept his head tilted, but his eyes monitored all human activity before him. A short line of customers waited their turn at the Apple store on the right. A young woman pushing a stroller encouraged the boy at her side to keep up. A large man with tattoos on his neck studied the contents of a luggage store window.

Frank noticed a woman wearing a gray suit strolling toward him on the other side of the second-story walkway. Her gaze hovered on Frank for a moment longer than he expected, and then she looked hastily away. Frank turned right on a bridge across the atrium that put him on an interception course with the woman, but before he reached her, she abruptly entered a novelty store.

What?

The woman's conservative appearance was a poor match for the store's target market, and Frank concluded she was likely a tail. He entered one of the anchor stores and hurried through the aisles of various departments. Coming to the store's center, he rode the escalator down one level and then up two levels. On the third floor, he re-entered the atrium, convinced that he had lost the woman, but hundreds of shoppers crowded the mall. A whole team could be on him, and he might not spot them. Was that guy at the phone case kiosk shopping or merely standing there? Why was the woman in office attire watching Frank from inside a lingerie store?

He took the next exit from the mall into the open parking lot and then crisscrossed through rows of parked cars toward another mall entrance. Halfway across the lot, he paused to turn a slow circle and scrutinized every person in view. No one showed him the slightest interest. But a clever enemy would have hung back to watch him through the tinted windows. On the other hand, maybe it was nothing. Maybe it was only his paranoia.

In any case, he had certainly lost the first tail, so he re-entered the mall feeling he had a fifty-percent chance of getting away clean. Frank wore a heavy coat with a big inside pocket for his Beretta. He juggled the packages and reached under his coat to flip off the safety.

Frank took the atrium escalator down and spent twenty minutes on a circuitous route through two more anchor stores, up and down more escalators, and finally back to his garage. Once inside the garage, he walked casually across the first level toward the staircase. A parked vehicle occupied every slot. Halfway to the stairs, a shoe scraped on cement, and

Frank turned. He reached for his gun but didn't see anyone. His heart rate jumped to the moon.

Frank hurried. He took the stairs up two levels, then cut diagonally across that level to another stairwell. From there, he tiptoed down to his story. His rental car was about fifteen spaces in. Frank strolled casually toward his car. When he was ten feet away, a man stepped out from a van at the far end of the floor and stared at Frank.

Frank raised his Beretta and fired, but the man jumped behind the van unscathed. Something moved near a truck on the right. Frank spun and fired in that direction. Two figures popped up from other locations and fired at Frank. Something tore at his sleeve, and Frank scurried to hide behind an SUV.

He gulped at the air, his heart beating like a drum roll. Frank lowered himself to the pavement and peered under the line of vehicles. A man's foot and ankle were on the other side of a car eight spaces down. Across the aisle, something moved between vehicles.

Darn.

"Frank," a man yelled. "It's no good. There are six of us on this level and another ten closing in."

Frank's lungs heaved. His eyes darted to the stairwell he'd come down, but he suspected they had a player lined up there to take a shot.

"Do the smart thing, Frank. Toss your gun in the open. We'll make a deal."

Jeez. These guys. Always with the deals.

He'd been approached a decade ago. Sell out your clients, and we'll ship you abroad. Money. New identity. Yeah, well, he'd done that on his own without taking a deal.

Frank pulled out his phone to study his favorite photo of Renée. They were sitting at the beach bar. The setting sun lightened her hair, and her eyes were smiling.

"We're running short of time," the man called. "You lit the fuse when you fired the first shot."

Frank typed a text, tweaked it a bit, and hit send.

I love you. Goodbye.

Frank figured his chance of getting away clean was less than one in a hundred. The odds of his former clients allowing him to survive a trial were even lower.

He'd never engaged in senseless killing. There had always been a reason. Money, he realized, was not a justification, but it was a reason.

Here, in this garage, why should he kill one or more of those hunting him? They would get him in the end anyway. Some of these guys had romantic partners. Some had children. What right did Frank have to deprive others of love for no reason?

"I'm coming out," he said. "Don't shoot."

Frank stood and stepped into the garage thruway. He held the Beretta at his side.

The same man emerged from behind the van. Frank guessed this was the man who had offered to make a deal. When the man saw that Frank was armed, he aimed his pistol. Others revealed themselves and pointed their handguns at Frank.

A chorus of stressed voices shouted. "Drop your weapon."

Frank walked toward the man in the driveway. An easy stroll. His breath was calm. His heart rate had slowed when he savored Renée's beauty. Many people never experienced the joy he had known when he took that photo.

The voices kept yelling. Frank recognized fear in the voices. They were afraid of being hurt, and they were afraid of hurting Frank. They should have listened to their training. He had already given them permission, but he was glad they hesitated. He wanted to get closer. It was hard for anyone to hit a live target with a pistol, particularly when the shooter's hands were shaking. The only way to reduce the margin of error was to get closer. Frank wanted to make it easy for them. Super easy. No mistakes.

The man seemed prepared. He held his pistol with two hands, but the barrel quivered. Frank was less than twenty feet away now. The voices faded into the background.

And Frank raised his pistol.

FIFTEEN

After the interview with Nikki, Bill called Kent Olsen to tell him of Cassandra Key's murder. Olsen's phone stayed silent for the longest time, and when he finally spoke, he sounded shaken. Olsen knew Cassandra had gone missing but was sure she'd turn up. Bill said the police had begun their investigation and asked whether they could stop by Olsen's place later to ask a few questions.

"Of course," Olsen had said. "Can you come in an hour?"

Olsen was staying at a rental unit in the Highlands complex on the same ridge where Bill lived. When Bill shared that news with Mitch Gentry, they exchanged a long, hard look. If Ms. Key was shot from the front, the killer must have fired their rifle from higher on the hill, and the Highland condos were directly above the chairlift station.

This could be a short investigation indeed.

But there might be many good vantage points where the killer could have stood, so Bill suggested they investigate the terrain on their way to Olsen's condo.

Their first stop was the overlook off of Wintergreen Drive. Mitch steered the squad car onto the pristine white blanket covering the parking lot. Bill and Mitch then trudged through eight inches of fresh snow to reach the covered observation deck that provided a stunning view.

It was a world of gray and white. The cloud cover had risen higher, but the sun had not yet broken through. The wind had died down, and it was eerily quiet. Snow covered everything—the hillside, the hollow before them, and the distant mountains. The air was sharp and clean. Several forensics team members were visible a quarter of a mile down the hill.

"What do you think?" said Bill.

Mitch shook his head. "I'm no rifle expert, but it seems a long way off. Also, you'd have to aim through a set of trees here and more trees in front of where she stood. Plus, we're not far from the road. It would be risky for the killer to take the shot from here."

"I agree. Do you know that wooden platform on the Highlands Leisure Trail? Maybe that's a better vantage point."

Mitch pursed his lips. "It's certainly closer. Let's check it out."

Another couple hundred yards up Wintergreen Drive, Mitch pulled into the driveway that led to the Highlands Express chairlift's upper station. The lift station was silent because the ski run remained closed for the investigation. Mitch parked the squad car at the yellow blaze that marked the Highlands Leisure trail. The undisturbed snow indicated they were the first to venture into the woods since the storm. They trod carefully because the course was uneven, and the snow made it challenging to avoid loose rocks. After they had gone a hundred feet, it seemed to Bill they were bush-whacking through the wild. But then he spotted the next trail blaze, and they soon reached the wooden platform. It was twenty feet square and covered with snow.

Bill and Mitch surveyed the scene. From the chairlift station on their left, cables bellied down to the first support tower. Law enforcement personnel stood under the chairlift several football fields away. He imagined a shooter with an aimed rifle lying prone on the platform.

Mitch turned to examine the hillside above them. "We're definitely hidden from clear view, but there are still some trees in the way. It would take one heck of a marksman to shoot her from here."

"Yeah, let's check out the view from the Highlands condos."

K ent Olsen was slender and taller than Mitch, probably six foot three inches. He had a high forehead and curly brown hair. His eyes were a soft blue and tinged pink. After greeting them at the door, he gave Bill a weak hand-shake and turned to walk back into the condo. Olsen offered them seats on a couch and sat in a nearby armchair. Wearing a sweatshirt, jeans, and socks, his body appeared drained of energy.

"I'm sorry for the loss of your colleague," said Bill.

And former lover, Bill thought, *but I won't lead with that.*

Mitch expressed his condolences, and Bill surveyed the large living area. Two coffee cups sat side by side on the breakfast counter next to the kitchen.

Olsen drew a shaky breath, then shook his head. "I'm having a hard time believing it. I saw her two days ago, larger than life. She was going to go hiking yesterday. What happened?"

"That's what we're trying to sort out," said Bill. "Nikki Churchill mentioned that your fiancée joined you yesterday."

"Yes, Elsie arrived in the afternoon."

"Is she here?"

"No. Elsie had an appointment with the Nature Foundation director. They're discussing trees, no doubt. She doesn't even know Cassandra is gone."

Bill's heart rate began to gather speed. Now he would shift from nice guy to inquisitive detective, and it wouldn't take Olsen long to realize he was a suspect, perhaps their prime suspect.

"Can you tell me where you were yesterday morning?"

Olsen's eyebrows furrowed, and his eyes rolled from Bill to Mitch.

"I was here. I worked here in the condo yesterday. I had planned to ski in the afternoon, but the storm came, and the resort shut down the mountain."

"So, you didn't see Ms. Key yesterday?"

Olsen drew his shoulders back. "Wait. Am I a suspect?"

Bill gave Olsen a nonchalant shrug. "We're gathering facts at this point."

Olsen's face remained cloudy, and he chewed on the inside of his lip, perhaps deciding whether now was a good time to call a lawyer. But calling a lawyer would make him appear guilty, a notion that may have occurred to Olsen, because he said, "I was here, working. I made notes for a presentation at the State Department. I have pages and pages of notes I can show you." He jumped up to fetch a legal pad from a side table and thrust them at Mitch.

Mitch courteously examined the handwritten notes.

But, of course, he could have written those notes anytime, days earlier, or even after he shot Cassandra Key.

"Do you work at the State Department?" said Bill.

"Yes. I have for fifteen years, ever since graduate school."

"I understand that you and Ms. Key were romantically involved at some point," said Bill.

Olsen cocked an eyebrow. "Who told you that?" But then he nodded. "Ah, Nikki. Not many people knew of our relationship, but it wasn't a big secret. We broke up three years ago."

"Would you call it an amicable separation?"

The State Department veteran rubbed his hands on the tops of his thighs. "Amicable? Yes. We're both adults. It wasn't my choice, but what could I do? And now I'm engaged to Elsie. Life goes on."

Bill nodded to signal he understood, then shifted gears. "Ms. Key died not far from here. Did you know that?"

Olsen crossed his arms and took far too long to answer the question. "No. You haven't told me the specifics."

"She was shot on the Wild Turkey ski run under the chairlift."

"Shot?" Olsen's eyes cut to the balcony doorway, as if the murder might be happening right now.

"Yes, she was shot with a rifle."

Olsen expressed even greater surprise at this revelation, and Bill asked if he'd heard or seen anything unusual around that time.

"No. I didn't hear a thing, but I listen to music when I'm working. And every time I looked out the door, the storm blocked the view."

Bill asked whether Olsen could think of anyone who would mean to cause Cassandra Key harm.

"Not to the point of murder. No. But Cassandra was argumentative. I always found her combative nature attractive, but it turned a lot of people off. She could be petty and vindictive. Honestly, Nikki was a saint to work for Cassandra these last three years."

"Do you have examples of her combative nature?"

Olsen gazed at the ceiling and then chuckled. "It's kind of funny, actually. I was thinking about the drones flying here to scout for the show. Cassandra hated drones and drone enthusiasts. She was at a sporting clay tournament once when a drone did a flyover to film the action. The drone was obviously not a sporting clay, but she shot it out of the sky. Cassandra claimed it was an accident, but no one believed her. Shooting at drones is illegal, but the police didn't press charges. The operator could have sued Cassandra, but he settled down when I insisted that she pay for the lost drone."

"Did the operator make any threats?" asked Mitch.

"No."

Though Olsen's observation was interesting, Bill couldn't see a connection with their investigation. The loss of a drone was hardly a motive for murder, particularly considering Key had made good the loss.

Bill suggested they step onto Olsen's balcony to assess the view. When he pointed to the crime scene, Kent Olsen gasped.

"There? She was shot there?"

"Yes," said Mitch. "Twice."

Although it was a long way off, they had a clear line of sight from the balcony to the crime scene.

"How difficult of a shot would that be to make from here?" asked Bill.

"From here?" exclaimed Olsen.

"Yes, from here."

Olsen swallowed hard and backed away from Bill. A panicked expression took over his face. "I didn't shoot Cassandra. I had no reason to. I liked her. At one point in my life, I loved her."

"We're not accusing you," said Bill, in an attempted neutral tone. "But can you answer the question?"

Olsen grabbed the balcony railing with his bare hands, ignoring the ice-cold metal. He stared at the site of Cassandra's death and said flatly, "It must be four hundred yards. Maybe more. It would be pure luck for me to make that shot. And you said she was shot twice." Olsen shook his head. "Never happen."

"Do you know anyone who could?" said Bill.

Kent Olsen nodded. "Yeah. Bryan McCasland, our treasurer. I'm only a hunter. I don't participate in high-powered rifle competitions, but Bryan does. Bryan's the best shot in the club."

Back inside the condo, Bill figured they'd gotten as much as they could from Kent Olsen at that point, but then Kent said he'd thought of something else.

"Back when we were together, Cassandra told me a story, only half a story, actually, but I remember it because it sent chills down my spine. She said an old man tried to get the best of her once, but she had tricked him. According to her, many people were afraid of this guy, but she wasn't. She said he was just an old man."

"Who was this person?" asked Bill.

Olsen shook his head. "When I asked her, she claimed she'd said too much already. So, I don't know for sure, but I have an idea. Four years ago, the transition of the club presidency from Allen Steele to Cassandra was apparently contentious. I gather Steele wanted to stay on, but Cassandra outmaneuvered him. Neither of them mentioned the conflict to me. I picked it up here and there from other members."

"Do you believe Allen Steele would drive up here to shoot Cassandra?" said Bill.

"No, he's too old. I suppose he could have paid someone to do it."

"That's interesting," said Bill. "Anything else?"

Kent Olsen had nothing to add, so Bill and Mitch made to leave. After standing, Mitch asked Olsen if he planned to leave Wintergreen anytime soon.

"Why? Are you asking me to stay?"

"That'd be nice, thanks. Just in case we have any follow up questions."

Outside in the squad car, Bill sent Krista Jackson a text asking her to track down Allen Steele. Then, Bill and Mitch exchanged their views of Kent Olsen. Mitch didn't trust him. Bill agreed that Kent had appeared suspicious, particularly his reaction when he first realized he was a suspect. But they were a long way from proving anything. They could get a warrant and search the condo, but Olsen was smart enough to have cleaned and moved his rifle. No, they would take the investigation one step at a time, and the facts would come forth as they always did, some willingly, others not. Mitch signaled his agreement but was still bothered by Olsen's demeanor.

"He's hiding something," said Mitch. "That's for sure."

SIXTEEN

Krista Jackson's fingers hovered over her keyboard as she listened to the caller through a headset. Four residents had reported hearing explosions in the Highlands area, and a fifth was on the line. But several of the callers believed they had heard firecrackers. This happened occasionally in Wintergreen, as some residents kept leftover fireworks from New Year's Eve and set them off whenever the mood struck them. Krista asked the caller if that's what he might have heard.

"No, miss. These were not firecrackers," the caller said. "I've been on the firing range enough times to know the difference. For your reference, I served as the Wintergreen Sporting Club's rifle-pistol team lead for several years."

Despite the dicey weather of the previous day, the caller, Major Bernstein—retired USMC—had taken his regular morning walk. He and his wife lived on Devils Knob Loop, and his exercise ritual was to hike a three-mile meandering route, including the portion of Blue Ridge Drive that passed the condo buildings.

"My wife told me I was crazy stubborn to go out yesterday. You know what I told her?"

Krista's knee bobbed impatiently. "Uh, no. What did you tell your wife, Major Bernstein?"

"Here's what I said to her. 'If I don't exercise, I'll get fat. When I get fat, you'll leave me for some other guy. Then where the heck will I be?'" Major Bernstein laughed so hard Krista turned the volume down on her headset.

"Where were you when you heard the rifle shot?"

Bernstein returned to business in an instant. "I had just crossed Blue Ridge Drive from the Shenandoah Ridge side into the Cliffs condos. I always pass through their parking lot because it's more interesting than the road. I was halfway down the first building when a rifle fired two shots in rapid succession. I'd say no more than a second apart, which is unusual for rifle shooting. They came from the other side of the condo buildings."

The hairs on Krista's nape tingled. The area Bernstein described was near where Cassandra Key had been shot.

"What time was that?"

"Let's see. I left the house around eleven fifteen. So, the shots were fired at eleven thirty, give or take ten minutes."

Krista typed a note in her file.

Then Bernstein said, "I sure hope you find that missing hiker. I can't imagine being out in the open last night."

Krista sat straight in her chair. She had forgotten for a moment that they were keeping news of the murder from the public. But that wouldn't last long. Secrets never kept on the mountain.

She thanked the major, ended the call, and consulted her notes. She'd worked emails and calls for two hours, and this was her first solid lead. In addition to statements related to explosions, she had received four drone reports from that side of the mountain. Most people had only heard a drone, but one reported a visual sighting in the area. Krista had half expected reports of drones because she had seen a drone on her drive up the mountain that morning. The drone had led her up Wintergreen Drive for several hundred yards as if showing her the way. But when they encountered a snow plow coming in the opposite direction, the drone peeled off. Krista considered them harmless.

The visual drone sighting came from Mrs. Spooner, who lived in the same building as Bill O'Shea. Mrs. Spooner reported by email that she had seen a larger drone than the others she'd noticed since the production company began preparing for the upcoming show. This drone had flown out of a low-hanging cloud, hovered near the Highlands Express lift, and then disappeared again. Given that Bill knew Mrs. Spooner, Krista decided to report the lead to him in case he wanted to follow up in person.

Krista fielded calls and emails for another hour and then noticed Mitch and Bill O'Shea entering the small police building. After their interviews, they had spent time with the forensics team at the murder scene. Krista reviewed the leads she had received with Bill and Mitch, then asked if they had learned anything of interest.

Bill and Mitch exchanged knowing glances.

"What?" said Krista.

"Kent Olsen is staying at the Highlands condos," said Mitch. "He has a clear line of sight to the murder scene from his balcony."

They kicked that subject around a bit, and then Bill glanced at his watch. "I need to get going. I'm watching Frieda Chang's dog for a few days. I'll check with Phyllis Spooner after I take Curly out for a break."

At that moment, Kerry, the other on-duty communications

officer, entered the aisle next to Krista's cubicle. "Hey, guys. A man has just come in who wants to report something. His name is Art Rossi."

Mitch gazed over the cubicle field toward the building entrance. "Isn't he the guy who gave us a key lead in the Susskind murder investigation?"

"Yeah," said Bill. "Let's hear what he has to say."

~

The four of them sat around the conference room table —Bill, Mitch, Krista, and Art Rossi. Rossi was a thin man in his fifties with dark hair and sharp eyes.

"I don't know whether this is related to your information request because it didn't happen in the Highlands Express area, but it was strange in a way that's hard to describe, so I decided to report it."

Bill nodded. "Thanks for stopping by."

"Have you ever hiked up the Lower Shamokin Falls trail?" said Art.

"I know it," said Mitch.

Bill had never hiked that particular trail but knew it began in Rockfish Valley and climbed up to Shamokin Falls.

"I had planned to do the hike yesterday," said Rossi. "It's a three-and-a-half-mile round trip with an elevation climb of eight hundred feet, so it's a decent workout."

Decent workout? Bill thought. *More like exhausting.*

"I knew the storm was coming, but the weather is never as bad in the valley, and I thought I could get the hike in. Anyway, when I reached the end of Old Stoney Creek Road, a truck and trailer were parked at the gate. That's the first thing that struck me as odd. I don't know why someone would park a trailer there. Never seen one before."

"What time was this?" said Mitch.

"About ten forty-five."

"Describe the truck and trailer," said Bill.

Rossi rubbed his chin. "The truck was a white F-150. The trailer was a plain flatbed eighteen feet long with some cabling on the back, like the driver had tied something down for hauling but then unloaded it."

"Did you see the driver?" said Mitch.

"No."

"I don't suppose you took a photo or remember the plates," said Mitch.

Rossi shook his head.

"You said the trailer was the first strange thing," said Bill.

"Yes," said Rossi, but then he hesitated, unsure how to proceed.

Bill waited patiently.

"This next part is going to sound weird. I'm not usually into sixth-sense stuff. Anyway, here goes. Once past the gate, I hiked the jeep road about half a mile until I reached the Peggy's Pinch substation. A hard snow was falling, and the ground quickly turned white. I hiked around the pump station and started to cross the pedestrian bridge over Stoney Creek."

Bill gave Rossi a nod of encouragement. Mitch sat back with his hands in his lap as if he had all the time in the world. Krista studied her fingernails.

Rossi scratched his neck. "I'll never forget the sight from the bridge. The trees were white with snow and arched together above the trickling stream. It was so beautiful that I paused in the middle of the bridge to take it in. But then a fierce wind blew snow at my face, and I made a snap decision to turn around."

"What exactly made you turn around?" said Bill. "The snow?"

Art Rossi sniffed, then shook his head. "No, it wasn't the weather. When the wind picked up, my scalp prickled. That never happens to me, but yesterday, standing in the middle of the bridge, I couldn't shake the notion that someone was watching me. The clouds had come low, and it was spooky standing above the stream." Rossi shuddered. "I can't describe it exactly, but I suspected that if I kept hiking up that trail, I would never come back again. I was a kid at the end of a ghost story, and I hauled ass back down the trail."

"But you never saw anyone?" said Mitch.

"No. I got in my car and drove away from there. I didn't breathe easy until I made it to Route 151."

Krista and Mitch asked a few clarifying questions but didn't get anything new. After Rossi left, Mitch asked Bill, "What did you make of that?"

Bill lifted his hands. "I don't know. Maybe nothing. Maybe the driver was up there drinking in the woods and heard Art coming. He watched Art from behind a tree, and Art got the spooky-wookies."

"Spooky-wookies?" said Krista. "What's spooky-wookies?"

"It's like getting spooked but worse," said Bill.

"Huh," said Mitch. "Spooky-wookies. Never heard of that."

"I made it up," said Bill. "Anyway, we tuck Art's statement away, and maybe it makes sense later. Maybe not. In any case, I've got to give Curly a break."

SEVENTEEN

B ack at home, Bill took Curly out for exercise. The temperature had risen to thirty-five during the day, but as nightfall closed in, it dipped below freezing again. The snow was eight inches deep, and Curly couldn't get much exercise, so they stuck to the cleared parking lots. Back inside the condo, Bill texted Phyllis Spooner to check her availability, and she asked him to stop by.

"Come in, Bill," she said after opening the door. "It's cold out. Have a seat by the fire. Want some hot chocolate?"

"Are you having some?"

"Just made mine. The water's still hot."

"Yes, please."

With a warm mug in his hands, Bill sat on the couch, and Phyllis Spooner sat in a comfortable chair on the other side of the coffee table. A few feet to Bill's left, flames licked at the neatly laid wood in the fireplace. The hot chocolate delighted Bill's taste buds.

Phyllis was an attractive woman in her mid-seventies with styled gray hair and bright eyes. Bill first met her when she identified a black bear that had surprised Bill in the parking lot. The bear—Ms. Betsy—had frightened Bill so severely he dropped his coffee and danish, which Ms. Betsy gobbled in a few instants.

"Bill," Phyllis said, "I want to thank you again for helping me with that other thing."

"It was no trouble. To be honest, I enjoyed the excitement."

"Thank you all the same."

Many years ago, when Phyllis was barely twenty, she enthusiastically participated in the hippie movement in California. Those were free-spirit days, and Phyllis signed up for the whole program. Rock 'n' roll. Protests. Drugs. Free love. She had done some things back then that she soon regretted. Then, many years later, in the fall season after Bill moved to Wintergreen, a man with no scruples discovered her past and blackmailed Phyllis. With some trickery, Bill convinced the man to return Phyllis's money and then delivered him—with incriminating evidence—to the police.

"Krista Jackson told me you reported seeing a drone yesterday morning," he said.

Phyllis raised her eyebrows. "Honestly, Bill, what's the point of having a policy prohibiting drones if it's not going to be enforced?"

"It's only until the show next week. The resort believes the show will generate excitement and a lot of business, which is good for all of us, right?"

Phyllis scrunched her nose, still skeptical. "I guess."

Bill related that the police had discovered the body of the missing hiker. She'd been murdered on the Highlands Express ski slope, and Bill was assisting with the investigation, which was why he had stopped by.

Of course, Phyllis was shocked at the news and anxious to help in any way she could.

"When I first heard the drone yesterday," she said, "I didn't take special notice because it seems like they're everywhere. But this drone was different."

"How so?"

"It was bigger. About the size of a dining table for six. And it carried some sort of payload."

"Payload?"

"I couldn't see it properly because it was too far away, but it was definitely carrying something."

Bill asked Phyllis to describe the precise location of the drone. Phyllis had gone onto her balcony to check on the storm when the buzzing sound of drone propellers reached her ears. Clouds rushed across the face of the mountain, and visibility changed often. At first, she couldn't see beyond the cliff's edge, but then the fog cleared enough to see as far as the ski runs, where a moving object caught her attention.

"It was down in the hollow, Bill, off to the left beyond the end of the condo buildings. The clouds were moving fast, and the drone dropped down from the clouds to zigzag across the black diamond ski runs." Phyllis moved her finger away from her body and back again to imitate the drone's path.

"How long did you watch it?" he said.

"Thirty seconds or so. Then a heavier cloud blocked my view."

"Did the payload resemble a package? Was it a delivery?"

Phyllis shook her head. "I didn't see it clearly. Something hung below the superstructure, but I don't think it was a box."

"Did you notice anything else? Hear anything?"

"No. But I had paused a movie to go outside. It was a James Bond film with lots of explosions. I turned the movie back on when I came in."

Bill pushed his lips out. The future was drones. He should

read up on them if they were going to become a constant in everyday life.

Phyllis didn't have anything else to add, but Bill wanted to ask a favor. Ever since he met with Nikki Churchill that morning, he'd worried about her. The combination of terrible news and a broken bone could knock anyone into a downward spiral. Phyllis had grown children of her own, including two daughters, and Bill asked if she would check on Nikki to make sure she was okay.

As he related his request, Phyllis's face filled with concern. "Absolutely," she said. "Give me her number. I'll call her right now."

Bill thanked Phyllis for the favor and the hot chocolate and made to leave.

At the door, she said, "It makes me nervous that there's a murderer loose on the mountain. I hope you catch this killer soon."

Bill nodded. "Me too."

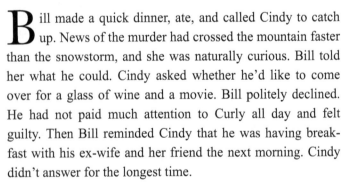

B ill made a quick dinner, ate, and called Cindy to catch up. News of the murder had crossed the mountain faster than the snowstorm, and she was naturally curious. Bill told her what he could. Cindy asked whether he'd like to come over for a glass of wine and a movie. Bill politely declined. He had not paid much attention to Curly all day and felt guilty. Then Bill reminded Cindy that he was having breakfast with his ex-wife and her friend the next morning. Cindy didn't answer for the longest time.

"You still there?" he asked.

"Yes. I had forgotten Wanda was coming."

Cindy's voice was filled with tension. Bill wished she

could relax. After all, Cindy had an ex-husband with whom she had raised two children. She knew how divorce worked. Though Bill and Wanda's marriage had ended, they no longer fought. They were friends now, good friends, and he looked forward to seeing her again.

After the call, Bill watched some television but kept yawning. Gosh, he was tired. In his dog bed at Bill's feet, Curly lay on his side with his eyes half closed and his legs hanging over the bed's edge. Bill envied Curly's ability to transition from an excited state to comatose and back again in a few short minutes. Bill should take him out once more before they both hit the sack for good.

"Come on, boy. Let's see what's going on outside."

In an instant, Curly was up. After shaking his body from head to toe, he trotted to the door and waited patiently for Bill to attach his leash. Outside, they turned the corner and tromped through the snow to the slope's edge. A million stars shone, brighter in Wintergreen than they would be if encumbered by the ambient light of a city. Over on the Blackrock side, bright spotlights illuminated the ski slopes. The High-lands Express area was dark, and a tiny green light hovered above the upper lift station. The green light moved down the ski slope and then drifted toward Bill. The drone's buzz reached Bill's ears.

The killer had most likely planned the murder in advance. They had known Cassandra Key would hike that morning, but how had they found her in the middle of a snowstorm? A notion crossed Bill's mind. Could the killer have used the drone Phyllis spotted to locate Cassandra and then shot her with a rifle?

He inhaled crisp air deep into his lungs and then shook his head. If he didn't stop thinking about the investigation, he'd never get a good night's sleep.

Curly pawed at the snow, sniffed, and pawed some more, clearly interested in something. Bill realized they were standing on top of Mr. Chips's burrow. During the prior summer, Bill had taught the neighborhood groundhog— whom he had nicknamed Mr. Chips—to eat tomatoes from his hand. Now, Mr. Chips slept comfortably in his burrow, fat from gorging on copious greens and ripe tomatoes well into the fall. And what of Ms. Betsy? Where did she slumber that night? Bill envied them, unburdened by the images of a murder in white.

EIGHTEEN

B ill's heart skipped a beat when he spotted Wanda coming down the hallway toward the Terrace Café in the Mountain Inn. Wanda was five foot three, with boundless energy that he had always considered a perfect match for her auburn curls. She and her friend, Amy Gallagher, were both dressed in jeans and sweaters. Amy wore huge glasses and had short red hair and a round face.

Bill and Wanda exchanged polite hugs. In stark contrast, Amy gave him a monster hug and held his face in her hands. "Gosh, O'Shea, it's great to see you. I can't believe you're living in the middle of absolutely nowhere. It is beautiful, though, covered in all this fresh snow."

A wide smile crept onto Bill's face, an involuntary reaction to the life force that was Amy. Amy possessed an abundance of enthusiasm for life's absurdities and was a font of knowledge on many topics. She read voraciously but also watched hours of cable news and reality television. Bill had never known a dull moment in her presence.

They ordered coffees and breakfast from the bar and then sat at a table near the lounge's gas fireplace. Outside, the sun had risen on a bright and warmer morning that seemed to put everyone in a good mood. The room was crowded and noisy with customers dressed in ski apparel, absorbing caffeine and calories before heading out to the slopes.

Wanda and Amy told Bill of their arrival the previous evening and their subsequent encounter with drone company employees at the Edge.

"Lord, Bill," said Amy, "those drone guys were so lonely we *had* to stop and chat with them."

Wanda laughed.

Bill said, "That doesn't sound bad."

"They were appreciative, to say the least," said Amy. "Or perhaps they were desperate. They kept ordering another round. Things were starting to get out of control. Then, as we were about to leave, one of them proposed to Wanda."

"Oh, shush," said Wanda.

Like Wanda and Bill, Amy was divorced, and she often complained that her love life lacked pizzazz. She raised her eyebrows and looked askance at Wanda. "I was invited to attend an upcoming drone conference, an offer I will seriously consider. Just saying."

"How were the roads coming in?" said Bill, to switch subjects. Discussing love lives with Wanda struck him as awkward territory.

"Not bad until we got here," said Wanda. "The plows had cleared most of the road coming up the mountain, but there were still icy patches."

"Will you two try skiing today?"

Amy wrinkled her nose. "Do I wish to break my leg in a vain attempt to have fun? No, thank you."

Wanda smiled. "We're going to visit the tubing park later. Want to join us?"

An image flashed in Bill's mind of Wanda and him

rushing down a snow-covered hill in inner tubes. At the end of the ride, Wanda popped up, laughed heartily, and threw her arms around his neck. They had never skied together, but for more than a decade, they had kept a pleasure boat at a marina. They had taken the boys wakeboarding and water skiing many times. Joining Wanda and Amy at the tubing park sounded fun, but he had other plans.

Plans to catch a killer, he thought.

But he didn't mention that. The police had not announced the murder to the public. Word had spread among locals on the mountain, but Wanda must not have heard, or she would have said something.

"Sorry, I can't," he said. "But we're still on for dinner tomorrow, right? I made reservations."

Wanda confirmed their dinner date, and the conversation moved to other topics. Bill and Wanda had two sons in their mid-twenties, and Amy's daughter was twenty-six. They discussed their children for a while, and then Amy brought up something she'd seen on a cable news show that morning.

"Did you see that story about the shooting in northern Virginia?" she said.

"No, I missed it," said Bill. He rarely watched cable news. Little good came from it that he could see.

Amy leaned forward and thrust her hands out for emphasis. "It was insane. They had a shootout in a shopping mall parking garage."

Wanda frowned. "I didn't see that."

"You were in the shower, and I forgot to tell you. It was an honest-to-goodness shootout. FBI agents were there, plus the local police. Apparently, they killed the bad guy, and get this—he was a professional hit man." Amy gave the last two words extra weight and then nodded solemnly.

Wanda asked which mall, and Amy named it. Then Amy

said she had shopped at that mall once, as if that lent her story even greater importance. Bill was relieved that no law enforcement personnel were injured.

Soon after that, Amy excused herself to visit the restroom. Wanda studied Bill's face with interest.

"What's going on?" she said. "You seem distracted."

"Nothing special. Some stuff up here. Not a big deal."

"Liar. Are you going back to work? I can always tell when something is up because you start fidgeting."

"I'm not fidgeting."

Wanda suppressed a giggle.

"Okay. There is something." Without going into great detail, Bill shared that he was helping out on a murder investigation.

Wanda grew still, and all of the humor left her face. "You're supposed to be retired. I know you're just helping out, but you must promise to be careful."

Bill nodded. "I have no intention of getting hurt. If something dangerous comes up, I'll leave it for the real cops."

NINETEEN

Deputy Chief Emily Powell, Mitch Gentry, Krista Jackson, and Bill met in the conference room for a scheduled video call with the ME, Soren Larsen. Arnie Shields from the sheriff's office also joined the call. After minimal pleasantries, Larsen began.

"The forensics team worked all day yesterday in freezing temperatures—not an ideal situation, I can assure you."

Arnie Shields chewed gum. He motioned with his hand, urging Larsen to cut to the chase.

"Then my team worked late into the night to perform the autopsy," said Larsen.

"Yes," said Arnie. "The citizens of Nelson County appreciate the hard work you and your team do to maintain justice in the land. Now, if we could get to the highlights."

"Hmpf," said Soren.

Not to be outdone, Emily said, "Let me assure you, Soren, that the Wintergreen Police Department is also grateful for your hard work. If you, or any member of your team, wants to visit us on a day off, I'm sure we could arrange complimentary lift tickets."

Soren Larsen's countenance brightened noticeably. He nodded. "Thank you, Emily. That's most considerate." Soren picked up a piece of paper and adjusted his glasses. "Now, let's see here. We have some interesting results. First, my initial assessment was correct: Ms. Key was shot twice in the chest with high-caliber bullets. At the time of the shooting, Key was standing and facing uphill. The killer must have fired the shots in rapid succession because the blood splatter and body position indicate she was still standing when the second bullet struck her."

In Bill's mind, he imagined Cassandra Key hiking Loggers Alley Trail across the hill. Then, she stopped and turned to face the slope above her. Why? What did she see? Hairs stood on the back of Bill's neck. Had she known that Kent Olsen was staying in the Highlands Condos? Had she seen Olsen on his balcony?

"Hold on," said Arnie. "When you say the killer fired the shots in rapid succession, what do you mean? Several seconds apart?"

Soren shook his head. "Less time than that. No more than a second between shots, I'd guess. Here's how I believe it played out. When the first high-caliber bullet struck Ms. Key, it passed through her body. She stood still at that moment, but only for a moment, and then the loss of blood and life force caused her to fall. Given the two bullets' entry points and pathways, we know she was still standing when the second bullet struck her."

Arnie blinked several times. "I must say, Soren, that is astonishing. I'm no trophy hunter, but I've done my share of deer hunting, and I can tell you it's hard enough to line up a shot on a clear day. But to fire and hit a target twice in one second in the middle of a snowstorm? That would take one heck of a marksman."

"Nevertheless," said Soren, "that's what the evidence indicates."

Arnie shook his head.

Bill said, "Have you been able to determine the location from which the shots were fired?"

"Not yet," said Soren. "I've called the Richmond office for help. They have a specialist in trajectories."

"What about the time of death?" said Emily.

Soren shrugged. "The conditions are not ideal, so I can only give you a wide range. She died sometime between eight o'clock and noon."

Arnie groaned. Bill said nothing but had the same reaction. The estimated time of death was of little value.

Larsen then summarized other autopsy findings, which were unremarkable. Key was a healthy female in her late thirties and not under the influence of alcohol or other foreign substances when she died. She had consumed a light breakfast of cereal and coffee that morning. Now that the forensics team had finished their work on the mountain, they would focus on Ms. Key's condo unit. Larsen then signed off the call, leaving the local team to plan the next steps.

Emily asked Bill to relate to Arnie what he and Mitch had learned from their interviews thus far.

Bill nodded toward Mitch. "Mitch, you summarize our findings. I'll jump in if I have anything to add."

Mitch glanced from Bill to Emily, perhaps unsure of where he stood. Bill wanted Mitch to become a better police officer, and the best way for him to grow was through experience performing tasks like summarizing findings for his superiors.

Mitch cleared his throat and gave a clear and succinct report, including the names of those attending the Old Virginia Gun Club retreat with Cassandra. Mitch concluded by mentioning the clear line of sight Kent Olsen had from his balcony to the crime scene.

"Do you think he's the guy?" said Arnie.

Mitch scratched behind his ear. "I don't know. He claims he's not a good enough marksman to make a shot at that distance."

"He wouldn't admit to that. Would he?" said Emily.

"No," said Mitch. "But we don't have a clear motive for Olsen."

Arnie frowned. Emily pushed her lips out.

"Mitch is right," said Bill. "We need more data. Let us meet with the other logical suspects to see what pops up. We need to interview the treasurer, McCasland, and Olsen's fiancée. And we want to speak with the trustee emeritus too. Allen Steele. Even though he's not here, he could give us some useful background, and he might have a motive. By the way, Krista, have you made contact with Steele?"

Krista reported that Steele lived in a senior retirement facility but was not reachable at the moment. He was apparently traveling with his daughter. Krista had called the daughter's cell number but not yet reached her.

After a bit of back and forth, they decided on a plan. Mitch and Bill would continue interviewing potential suspects. Krista would do background searches on everyone involved. In addition, Krista would knock on every door in the Highlands Condos. If Kent Olsen fired a rifle from his balcony, someone else should have heard a noise. Arnie promised the support of the sheriff's office when they needed it and signed off.

On the way out of the conference room, Emily asked Bill to come into her office for a minute.

"Alex is beside himself," she said. "I gave him an update this morning, and he wanted to book the next plane back. I convinced him to hold on for twenty-four hours to see what developed. What's your view?"

Alex Sharp was the acting chief of police for the Wintergreen community and currently vacationing in Florida.

"Good advice," said Bill. "We have a short list of suspects and could wrap this up in a day or two. There's nothing he could do that you won't."

Emily nodded. "But you know Alex. He's always eager to do his share and then some."

"Want me to call him?" said Bill.

Emily bobbed her head as she weighed Bill's suggestion. "Yeah. That's a good idea. Call him at the end of the work day to let him know where you are."

"Never know. We might have the case gift-wrapped by then."

"Don't say that," said Emily. "You'll jinx it."

TWENTY

K rista arranged for Bill and Mitch to meet Bryan McCasland at the Pro Re Nata brewery on Route 250 outside Crozet. McCasland had a busy day planned, with a morning activity in Crozet and afternoon meetings in Charlottesville, but he agreed to meet them for an interview over lunch.

McCasland was five feet tall plus a few inches, slender, and had short brown hair and dark eyes. He met them inside the brewery and greeted Bill with a firm handshake. The brewery had a high ceiling, polished concrete floors, and enough wooden tables and chairs for a hundred customers.

Bryan had heard of Key's death and started the interview with expressions of shock and dismay.

He shook his head. "This is a terrible thing. I understand she was shot while hiking? Unbelievable. That means she was murdered, doesn't it?"

"I'm afraid so," said Mitch.

Several customers had taken note of Mitch's uniform, but no one displayed much of a reaction. Generally speaking, Mitch adopted a casual bearing in public. McCasland's eyes flitted back and forth between Mitch and Bill. They settled on Bill.

"What's your role in this?" he asked.

"I'm a retired police detective who happens to live in Wintergreen. The deputy chief asked me to help out on the investigation, a temporary thing. Can you tell us where you were Friday morning?"

McCasland nodded. "Sure. Yeah. Cassandra invited us up here for a retreat. The whole thing's been a bit of a pain. We were supposed to come last week, but her schedule changed, and she pushed it back. So, I had to rearrange a lot of stuff. Anyway, that day was supposed to be leisure time on the mountain, but I had to work. I do procurement for the Air Force. We have a big project out to bid, and I spent the morning reading proposals."

"Where are you staying?" said Mitch, as if he was asking out of idle curiosity.

"The White Oak Townhomes. They're near the Mountain Inn."

Mitch nodded.

Mitch may have noted, as did Bill, that the White Oak location was a short distance from the Highlands Leisure trail they had visited the previous day. McCasland could have easily stood on the wooden platform and spotted Key hiking on Loggers Alley.

"Did you speak to anyone in the morning?" said Bill. "Maybe on a video conference call?"

McCasland shook his head. "No, I spent most of the time reading."

A server stopped by the table to ask if they wanted anything. McCasland requested a cup of water. Bill and Mitch said they might order food later.

Bill wondered how long it would take McCasland to hike

to the wooden platform, shoot Cassandra Key, and return to his condo. Twenty minutes? Could he have done that without attracting attention? Probably, given that everyone was focused on the weather.

"I understand that you participate in high-powered rifle competitions," said Bill.

McCasland raised his hands to slow Bill down. "Yes, that's true. It's my hobby. That's where I was this morning, over at Crozet Rifle and Pistol. But I didn't shoot Cassandra. I'll admit we had our disagreements, but I'm a businessman. Unlike Cassandra, I don't escalate. I negotiate. She only knew one approach to dealing with conflicts. Fire away. Fire away. Fire away."

"How is the club doing financially?" said Bill.

Bryan grimaced. "Terribly. We're going broke. Membership is way down, but our costs stay the same. Cassandra pretended we still had a thousand members paying five thousand a year. In reality, we're down to three hundred members and change."

"What's happened to membership?" said Mitch.

"They grew old, and now they're dying off or quitting. We have a hunting lodge in the western part of Virginia, and there was a time when local chapters booked that place every week of hunting season. Now, we're lucky to book it three or four times a year, but we still have a full-time caretaker. There are other mismanagement examples. I could go on and on."

McCasland's insinuation was easy to grasp. If he was in charge, things would be different. His ideas would save the organization. His open disdain for Cassandra Key lent him the appearance of a suspect, but McCasland couldn't resist carrying on.

"Here's another example of her disregard for the club's

dire straits. Allen Steele told me this story a few years ago. He was president of the club himself at one time. Now he's a trustee emeritus."

Bill nodded to show that he was aware of Steele and his position.

"When I first became treasurer, I reviewed the numbers and realized what bad shape we were in. Cassandra didn't wish to discuss the matter. She had a plan to stimulate membership, the same plan she'd pursued for a year without success. Anyway, I met with Steele to get his perspective. He agreed with my analysis and then told me this crazy story. Apparently, a wealthy man wanted to join the club once and offered to make a substantial donation to help shore up our finances. But Cassandra didn't like this guy, so the club denied his application."

"Why didn't Cassandra like him?" said Mitch.

McCasland shrugged. "I asked Steele for more details. I wanted to check out this person myself to see if we could revisit the matter because we definitely needed the money. But Steele wouldn't give me a name. Steele is over ninety years old and doesn't want to stir things up. Frankly, he's not much of a factor on the board. I'll expect he'll resign soon."

Mitch nodded and said, "Can you think of anyone who might have benefited from Ms. Key's death?"

McCasland answered immediately. "Elsie Dale, for one."

"Kent Olsen's fiancée? How so?"

"Do you know how Elsie and Kent met?"

Mitch and Bill shook their heads.

McCasland chuckled. "It's an amusing story. The Old Virginia Gun Club had hunting rights to a large landholding in southeastern Virginia. Miles of pine forests. Excellent deer hunting. But the Dale Lumber Company bought the land from the original owner and wanted to modify the hunting rights.

Even though we only had three years to go on the hunting lease, Cassandra—never one to compromise—said no to any changes, which was idiotic because the lumber company could afford to wait us out." Bryan shook his head in disgust. "She turned what should have been a simple negotiation into this big negative thing. It was embarrassing for everybody involved. Finally, Kent Olsen saw what was coming and reached out to the company to fashion a compromise. That's how he met Elsie Dale."

Bill pulled on his chin. Though he had never met Cassandra Key, the people he'd interviewed had portrayed a combatant who relished fighting more than victory. He decided he wouldn't have liked her much.

"I don't follow you," Mitch said to McCasland. "I get the conflict over hunting rights, but how does Ms. Key's death benefit Ms. Dale?"

"Ties up a loose end," said Bryan. "She's a billionaire, or close to it, and has political aspirations. She doesn't want her fiancé's former lover hanging around."

Bill ground his teeth.

Mitch said, "And you consider that a sufficient motive for murder?"

McCasland looked at Mitch and Bill as if he'd suddenly realized he'd said something wrong. "I guess not, but Elsie had good reason to be angry."

Angry? Perhaps. Enraged? Not likely.

Bill took a mental note to keep an eye on McCasland. The guy had strange beliefs concerning human behavior.

"Anyway," said Bryan, "I know Kent had high hopes for this executive retreat. Small group. Beautiful setting. Kent had wanted to broker peace between Cassandra and Elsie once and for all. But that was wishful thinking. Two women like that. Both headstrong. I always believed Kent would have to choose between working with Cassandra and his relationship with Elsie. But not now—the killer made the choice for him."

McCasland left soon after that, and Bill's mood improved markedly upon his departure. Some people gave off bad vibes without even trying. But it was sunny outside, and the brewery customers were in a festive mood. Bill craved a draft beer but would settle for an early lunch and a Diet Coke. He and Mitch perused the menu and then ordered. Bill opted for the salmon sandwich, and Mitch chose the Philly cheesesteak.

They had placed their orders and were discussing the McCasland interview when a tall blond woman approached.

"Is that you, Bill? I thought so."

It took Bill a moment to remember Tanya Stafford, a corporate executive he had met during the Damian Susskind investigation. Tanya was CEO of Fair Game, a sporting goods company based in Charlottesville. Fair Game specialized in outdoor sports: hunting, fishing, and camping. She joined Bill and Mitch at the table and explained that she was in the neighborhood because the company had sponsored a high-powered rifle competition at the Crozet Rifle and Pistol Club. As an avid hunter, Tanya had participated in the contest.

"How'd you do?" asked Bill.

"I came in third. A Crozet club member got second. I don't feel bad about losing to him—he practices shooting twice a week."

"Who won first place?" said Mitch.

Tanya's gaze turned toward the exit. "The guy you were chatting with, Bryan McCasland. He's a demon on the range."

Mitch scratched his temple. "Have you competed with McCasland other times?"

"Yeah. Bryan's a regular on the circuit. I'd say he's one of the top three shooters in the state."

Bill knew nothing of rifle shooting competitions. Did participants ever compete in adverse conditions?

"How do you guys know McCasland?" Tanya said.

Bill explained they were investigating the murder of an acquaintance of Bryan's.

Tanya nodded as if she now understood. "I heard about Cassandra. That's awful."

"Did you know Ms. Key?" said Bill.

"Oh, yes. I'm a member of the Old Virginia Gun Club. We had common interests as two female leaders in the male-dominated outdoor sporting world. But Cassandra could be intense, so I didn't hang out with her a lot."

Then Bill realized that Tanya Stafford could be of assistance. As a neutral party who was also a rifle expert, Tanya could assess the shot Kent Olsen would have had to make to kill Cassandra Key. So Bill asked Tanya whether she'd be willing to help out. Tanya said yes, but she had a packed schedule that afternoon, so they arranged to meet in Wintergreen the next day.

Tanya then smiled. "I understand you guys have some drones flying around in Wintergreen. I bet that pissed Cassandra off."

"Why do you say that?" said Bill.

Tanya chuckled and said Cassandra's hatred of drones was legendary.

Bill nodded. "I gather she once blasted a drone from the sky. Why did she hate drones?"

"To be fair," said Tanya, "many hunters are not keen on drones. I'll tell you why."

Drone technology continued to evolve rapidly, and hunters like Cassandra Key feared drones would change the traditional hunter's world by making game spotting effortless. Federal laws prohibited using drones for hunting, but rules were subject to change. Hunting was declining in the US, and managing wildlife like deer was growing more challenging. Cassandra could see a future when hunting would become little more than a video game.

Tanya finished her explanation, then paused and cocked an eyebrow. "It's weird that we're discussing Cassandra and drones right now."

"How's that?" said Mitch.

"Because she didn't just blast any drone from the sky. She shot down Chas Skibinski's drone."

Bill shrugged to indicate he didn't know the name.

"Skibinski owns the company putting on the drone show in Wintergreen."

"Seriously?" said Mitch.

Bill's mind raced ahead. Maybe they had another suspect after all.

"Uh-huh," said Tanya. "They call him the Drone King."

TWENTY-ONE

To Bill's surprise, when Krista contacted Elsie Dale to request an interview, Ms. Dale suggested they meet at the Wintergreen police station.

Elsie Dale was a beautiful young woman. Underneath her dark ski parka, she wore a royal blue sweater with a matching scarf tied at the neck. She had long dark hair and engaging brown eyes. Seated on the opposite side of the conference table, Elsie Dale examined Bill and Mitch with interest and then proceeded to scrutinize the four white walls of the room.

"I've never been inside a police station," she said. "I thought it might be interesting, but it's not, is it? It's not dingy, thank goodness, but the rooms are small and the interior design uninspired."

Bill smiled. "This one's not much different from others. I guess law enforcement puts a low priority on interior design."

"A pity," said Elsie Dale. "Have your chief contact me. For ten thousand dollars, I'll bring a budget designer in here for a few hours who will work miracles. I'll donate the money if you promise not to consider it a bribe."

Mitch glanced nervously at Bill, unsure of how to respond.

"Thank you for coming in," said Bill. "I'm sure you've heard of Ms. Key's passing by now. We're trying to ascertain what happened."

"You mean figure out who killed her," said Dale.

"Precisely," said Bill with a tight grin. "Perhaps you could start by describing your relationship with Ms. Key."

Elsie Dale frowned. "I didn't have a relationship with Cassandra Key. She meant nothing to me."

"Are you aware that she was at one time romantically involved with your fiancé?" said Bill.

With her forearms on the table, Dale slowly rubbed her hands together, supremely confident. "Yes, fine, Cassandra and Kent had an affair, but that ended years ago. I don't consider it relevant. I've had lovers too."

"When did you arrive in Wintergreen?"

"The day before yesterday. I drove up from Chesapeake."

In her following answers, Dale asserted that she had driven alone and stopped twice along the way, once for gas west of Richmond and then at a rest stop between Charlottesville and Crozet.

"How were the roads on the way up the mountain?" Bill asked.

"Awful. I could barely see the road, but I slowed to a crawl and managed."

Bill paused to ruminate. Elsie Dale observed him casually, not the least bit nervous. What did he hope to accomplish in this interview? He could hardly see Elsie Dale as a suspect. According to her statement, she wasn't here in time to commit the murder. Furthermore, she didn't have the marksmanship to pull it off. And as far as motive was concerned, Bill couldn't find one. But maybe she could shed light on other areas.

"When did you first learn of Ms. Key's death?" said Bill.

Elsie's eye twitched, the first sign that these extraordinary events had an impact on her.

"Yesterday afternoon, when I got back to the rental condo from a meeting. Kent told me."

"Did he appear upset?"

Elsie stared at her hands. "Yes, he did. He'd been crying when I got there. A natural reaction, I'm sure, from hearing that a long-time friend and former lover had been brutally murdered."

"Did he describe how Ms. Key was killed?"

Elsie tweaked her nose. "He didn't give me many details, just that she'd been shot by a rifle. Kent said the news made him sad and tired. He went into the bedroom to nap, but later, I heard him crying through the door. He's still upset."

Bill nodded. Even though they'd been divorced for years, if Wanda died suddenly, he would grieve for a long time.

"I gather there was a dispute over hunting rights between you and Cassandra. Can you tell us about that?"

Elsie Dale shrugged. "It wasn't a newsworthy dispute. The company bought the land and wanted to alter the harvesting schedule in a way that required changing the hunting rights. Cassandra didn't want to negotiate. Publicly, she tried to paint us as part of the anti-gun lobby, which was absurd. Privately, she tried to manipulate local regulations. She believed she had the county board of supervisors in her pocket, but she was wrong."

"That's it?"

"Yes. Listen, I didn't care for Cassandra because she used to be with Kent, and from a business perspective, she was a pain in the butt. But at the end of the day, she didn't matter enough for me to give it much thought. We own a lot more acreage in North Carolina, Georgia, and other southern states. I wrestle with bigger issues every day."

Bill checked with Mitch, but he didn't have any other questions, so Bill thanked Elsie Dale for coming in. After she left, Bill asked Mitch what he thought.

Mitch scrunched his eyebrows. "I wouldn't invite her over for dinner, but I can't see her as a likely suspect."

"I agree. Notice anything else?"

"The thing that bothered me was her nonchalance. She must realize her fiancé is still a suspect at this point, but she doesn't seem upset about it."

Bill smiled. He was pleased with Mitch's observation.

"What should we do?" asked Mitch.

"Follow up, so she knows she's still on our list. She said she bought gas west of Richmond. Find out what station and verify the transaction. The timestamp will solidify her alibi. Or not."

Mitch nodded.

"The magic is in the grunt work, Mitch. You never know what the details will turn up."

TWENTY-TWO

B ill drove up the mountain to take Curly out for a break. During their twenty-minute stroll around the tennis courts, Bill worried about the killer's shot. He couldn't make sense of it. Two shots from four hundred yards within a second. An approaching snowstorm. Poor visibility. High winds.

He tried to imagine Kent Olsen lying prone on his balcony. Wearing what? His workout clothes? Olsen checked the view through his rifle scope, spotted a hiker wearing orange, and lined up his shot. The wind howled. Snowflakes swirled onto his balcony and against his face. Kent wiped a hand across his eyes, sighted the target, and pulled the trigger. The shell casing ejected, and a second cartridge auto-reloaded. Kent sighted again and pulled the trigger a second time. Then, he scanned his surroundings to verify that no one had seen him, packed his gear, and hurried back into the condo.

No. It was a scene from a spy thriller. Kent Olsen had an office job writing position papers on diplomatic strategy. And Bryan McCasland? For crying out loud, he worked in logistics. No. Whoever killed Key had done this before. They had planned it down to the last detail and executed their plan with perfection. Key's murder bore the marks of a professional killer, and neither Olsen nor McCasland fit that description.

Professional killer.

A chime sounded in Bill's head.

That morning, when he had coffee with Wanda and Amy Gallagher, Amy had mentioned a sensational story from a cable news show. The FBI and local law enforcement engaged in a suburban shootout with a retired professional killer.

"Hurry up, Curly," Bill said. "We need to make a call."

As a homicide detective in Columbia, South Carolina, Bill had worked with the FBI several times. One former contact—who owed Bill a rather large favor—had moved up in the FBI organization and now worked out of DC. Bill called Skip Forrester and explained the situation.

"Ah, yeah, seems like you're grasping at straws," said Skip. "You're three hours from here in the middle of nowhere."

Bill frowned at Curly. The request had struck Bill as reasonable in advance, but when he delivered it to Skip, he sounded borderline desperate.

"I know the odds are long," said Bill, "but I'm not asking a lot. Read the situation report. Make a phone call or two. Throw me a bone."

"It's not a bone, dude. If I go poking into someone else's investigation, they'll want to know why."

"So, tell them."

"Then they'll think *I'm* the one grasping at straws."

Bill grimaced. "Skip, help me out here. How often have I called you in the past?"

"You called a few months ago with that blackmailing situation."

"That worked out okay for you. Didn't it? Maybe this will too."

Skip didn't answer right away. A light tapping sound made its way through the ether to Bill's ear. He imagined Skip drumming his desktop.

"Okay," Skip said. "I'll make a few calls."

"You're a rock star," said Bill. "Come visit Wintergreen sometime. I'll buy you dinner."

"Uh-huh."

And the phone went dead.

TWENTY-THREE

The Edge restaurant sported a ski-lodge-style interior with high ceilings, wooden tables and chairs, and early twentieth-century skis fastened to the walls for decoration. Televisions mounted behind the bar played NFL playoff games with the sound muted. Bill had rarely seen the Edge more crowded. Patrons occupied most of the tables and stools, and a couple dozen people stood in the open area near the bar.

Based on Amy and Wanda's report from their earlier visit to the Edge, Bill thought he'd try finding Chas Skibinski there. He approached a small group of casually dressed men and asked if anyone knew Skibinski.

One of the men said, "The Drone King? Sure." He scanned the room and pointed toward the bar. "That's him. The man in the black sweater speaking with the blond woman."

"Thank you."

Bill weaved his way through the crowd toward Skibinski and noticed the blonde sitting with him.

Oh, jeez. Of all the luck. Rachel Dunn.

Bill knew Rachel Dunn because of her involvement in another investigation. Earlier in life, Rachel had worked as a high-priced escort for the diplomatic market in DC, but she now offered services as a masseuse to customers in Wintergreen. Bill had been skeptical about Rachel's new endeavor, but she convinced him she ran it as a clean business with no off-menu services. Fair enough. Everyone deserved a second chance.

Rachel lived alone, and Bill had seen her at the Edge on other occasions. She apparently stopped by often to socialize with the staff—whom she knew well—and for the chance of meeting someone new. Sitting on a barstool facing Skibinski, Rachel spotted Bill as he approached. An attractive woman in her mid-forties, Rachel matched Bill's image of a yoga instructor. She wore a tight brown sweater, dangling earrings, and a black Apple watch.

Rachel smiled broadly. "Well, if it isn't Bill O'Shea. It's been ages. What brings you to the Edge?"

"Hello," Bill said, somewhat awkwardly. He shook Rachel's hand when she offered it. Her hand was warm and strong. "Sadly, I'm here on official business. But, given your connections on the mountain, you may have heard the news."

Rachel pulled her head back. "Oh, I *did* hear that. A woman was murdered, right? While she was hiking?"

Bill nodded and then glanced at Skibinski, who had waited politely on standby.

"Sorry," Rachel said, and she introduced the two men. She mentioned that Bill was a retired police detective who occasionally assisted the Wintergreen police department.

"So, you're working on the investigation into Ms. Key's death?" asked Chas Skibinski. He had gray eyes, curly red hair, and a carefully groomed three-day beard.

"Yes," said Bill. "How did you hear about it?"

"Ms. Key has a reputation with the drone community, so the news of her death spread quickly on social media."

A bartender stopped to check on their drinks, and Rachel asked Bill if he wished to order something.

"No, thank you," he said, and then he turned to Skibinski. "I understand you're in charge of the drone show preparations."

"That's right. This is my company's first big show. Normally, a place like Wintergreen couldn't afford the kind of show we're planning, but I needed a place to test my crew and the software. Wintergreen agreed to be a beta site if I gave them a substantial discount. While we're here, we're also shooting some marketing footage for the resort."

"Ah ha," said Rachel. "That's why we have all of these drones flying around."

Skibinski nodded. "It's exciting, but I'm taking a bath on the economics. To make matters worse, last month, the resort shifted the schedule back a week, which drove my costs even higher."

"Hey," said Bill. "I'm sorry to interrupt your conversation, Chas, but could I get a few minutes of your time? You might be able to help me with the investigation."

Skibinski's eyebrows lifted. "Sure. Here?"

Bill asked if they could go outside where it was quieter.

Chas stood to leave and said to Rachel, "Be right back. Guard this stool with your life."

The noise level dropped as soon as they stepped through the front door. They strolled toward the Mountain Inn, and Bill apologized again for interrupting Skibinski.

"No problem. How can I help?"

Bill explained that they had a report of a drone near the crime scene at the time of the murder. Could the killer have used a drone to find Ms. Key on the slopes?

Skibinski nodded. "Certainly. Drones have excellent camera capabilities. But, of course, the killer would need her description."

"Would that require a large drone?"

"No. Many small drones could handle the camera aspects. But the weather was terrible that day, right? High winds, low temperatures, and snow. Most drones don't handle those conditions well. In fact, I kept almost all of our drones on the ground."

Bill nodded. He began the interview with easy questions to warm the Drone King up before venturing into awkward territory.

"I understand you had a public dispute with Cassandra Key not long ago."

Skibinski burst out laughing. "Oh! Is that why you wanted to see me? Because Key shot down my drone?"

"I was curious, yes."

They reached the Mountain Inn patio and turned right to walk behind a row of wooden Adirondack chairs. Three men sat in the chairs smoking cigars.

Skibinski calmly explained Cassandra Key's problem with him and the drone world. To start, he reiterated the same points Tanya Stafford had made earlier. Managing deer and swine wildlife populations was challenging because fewer hunters were available to cull the herds. Drones could help state agencies solve these problems by making hunting more efficient. Being an ardent drone evangelist and an officer of the National Drone Society, Skibinski had approached Key to discuss this approach. Key soundly rejected his ideas. When asked why, Cassandra said the concept was a Trojan horse from drone manufacturers. Grant them this step, and soon, the sport would be taken out of hunting altogether.

"Cassandra feared that rich armchair gamers would eventually pay to hunt lions and elephants in Africa without ever leaving their playrooms."

Bill's stomach turned. "Is that a legitimate concern?"

"No," said Skibinski, with conviction. "There would be a huge outcry. Technically speaking, the drone-enabled culling of wild pigs will soon be feasible, but I can't see governing bodies ever approving it for sport hunting."

Bill wasn't sure. If the rich could buy a seat on an orbital spaceship, why couldn't they buy a trophy hunt on their television?

"In any case," said Chas, "my conversation with Cassandra Key ended badly. I admit that I became a bit obsessed with her. I flew several scouting flights over her retail stores. Then, when the Old Virginia Gun Club sponsored a sporting clays tournament, I heard about it and showed up. Cassandra realized I was flying a drone overhead and couldn't resist shooting it down. Honestly, it was laughable, her blasting a drone with a shotgun. I saw her afterward, and she was all flushed with excitement from the conflict. She loved fighting. I could sense that when we first met."

"Did you harbor ill feelings toward her?"

Chas shrugged. "Not really. It was my fault for being a jerk, and the manufacturer loved the incident. Free publicity."

"When did you last see Cassandra?"

"At the sporting clays tournament six months ago. I've steered clear of her since then. I didn't know Cassandra was here until the news of her death surfaced."

When they returned to the Edge, Skibinski excused himself to the restroom, and Bill stopped to see Rachel at the bar.

"Can you do me a favor?" he asked.

Rachel gave him a coy smile. "No free massages, Bill. Not even for you."

Heat rushed to Bill's face. Like few women he'd met, Rachel could unnerve him. He ignored her comment.

"Keep an ear open tonight," he said.

Rachel's eyes scanned the room. "You think there's a killer in this bunch?"

"No, I don't. But I'm in the market for tidbits. So please let me know if you hear anything of interest."

With a face full of mirth, Rachel gave him a sharp salute. "Count on me, detective."

And the heat rose to Bill's cheeks again.

TWENTY-FOUR

B ack at his condo, Bill called Cindy to catch up, hoping to finagle an invitation like the one he'd passed on the previous night. No such luck. Cindy said she was tired because she had worked late to prepare for an event she would cater the next day. Bill would have offered to lend a hand at the event, but he'd committed to Emily that he would see the investigation through. Bill and Cindy chatted for ten minutes and then ended the call.

Curly lay sprawled across his bed, one eye lazily open and the other closed.

"What do you say, Curly?" Bill said. "Will we sort this murder out? Yes, I agree. It's up in the air."

Several people had ongoing disagreements with Cassandra Key, but Bill doubted whether any of those conflicts would have driven a person to murder. And even if a drone spotted Key hiking, how did the killer make that shot? Skip Forrester was right—Bill was struggling to make progress.

Frieda Chang called on video and wanted to chat with Curly. Bill aimed his phone at Curly, and at the sound of Frieda's voice, Curly perked up and came to Bill. Frieda expressed her undying affection for the dog, and Curly offered a single bark in return. When Frieda asked if there was news on the mountain, Bill gave her a quick update on the Cassandra Key murder.

"Goodness, Bill," she said. "Maybe I should come home early. The last thing you need now is a dog to care for."

"Oh, no. Curly's no bother. He and I were kicking around some ideas for the investigation."

Frieda laughed, and they discussed her conference for a few minutes. Then she said goodbye, leaving Bill and Curly alone again. Bill glanced at the side table, where a science fiction novel he'd been reading called for his attention, but then he remembered his earlier resolution to research the world of drones. So he picked up his laptop and read articles concerning current and near-future applications. The possibilities were endless—package delivery, communications relay, crop management, and real estate marketing. Not to mention military weapons.

Bill's phone buzzed again. Skip Forrester, his FBI contact.

"Yeah," said Skip, after initial greetings, "this is interesting. Two days ago, a former FBI analyst recognized a man named Frank Richardi in a convenience store outside of Warrenton. In his prime, Richardi was a professional killer this analyst had followed closely. But Richardi disappeared years ago, and the FBI concluded he was probably buried in some obscure location."

"Okay."

Skip told Bill that Richardi flew into Dulles from Martinique under a different name the day before the analyst spotted him. Richardi rented a car and spent the night in a hotel near Dulles. The investigators had since contacted the auto rental company to retrieve the location history of Richardi's car. Apparently, after spending the night, Richardi had driven to Charlottesville.

"Charlottesville?"

"That's correct."

"What did he do in Charlottesville?"

"We don't know. We know the car sat in a parking lot for four hours. Then Richardi drove the car to Warrenton, where our former analyst spotted him in the convenience store."

Bill frowned, then said, "Do you still believe I'm grasping at straws?"

"No."

That an FBI shootout in a northern Virginia mall would be connected to Cassandra Key's death had seemed highly improbable. But now, they had a professional killer in Charlottesville on the date of Key's murder, and Wintergreen was only an hour away. Did Richardi somehow secure another vehicle, drive to Wintergreen, and shoot Key? Maybe he was a former sniper, which could explain the killer's accuracy.

"What else do you know about Richardi?" asked Bill.

"Not much. We have a file on him, but I haven't read it yet. I'll learn a lot more tomorrow. Of course, we don't know for sure that it was him."

"Right. He might have gone to tour Monticello. But if so, why didn't he take the car?"

"Exactly."

They kicked it around a while and divided up tasks. Skip would learn more about Richardi—clients, methods, current status, etc. Bill would send someone to the Charlottesville parking lot to poke around.

After his conversation with Skip, Bill sat on the floor and gave Curly a belly rub. Then he reached for his phone again and called Mitch Gentry.

TWENTY-FIVE

The next morning, Bill took Curly on his usual tour around the tennis compound. The previous day's sun had melted much of the snow, making their course less cumbersome for man and beast. Back at the condo, Bill prepared Curly's food, refilled his water bowl, and made ready to take a longer walk by himself. Then a knock sounded at the front door. Curly barked and came running, all excited at this new development.

Bill glanced at his phone. Seven fifty-five. Who could that be? He couldn't remember anyone visiting this early.

He opened the door to find Rachel Dunn.

Holy Peter, Paul, and Mary!

Rachel wore skinny white jeans, brown boots, and a pink puffer coat with a matching beanie cap. Her dark eyes sparkled with mischief.

Bill swallowed hard. His neck grew warm. He hadn't shaved and wore warmup pants, an old sweatshirt, and a ball cap.

"Good m-morning," he said.

Curly greeted Rachel warmly by wagging his butt and lifting his head in supplication.

Rachel crouched, allowed Curly to sniff her hand, and then scratched him behind the ears. "I didn't know you had a dog, Bill. I never pictured you as a dog person."

Bill explained that he was watching Curly for a friend.

Still standing in the doorway, Rachel said, "Well, are you going to invite me in or what?"

"Ah, my place is kind of a mess."

What is she doing here this early?

"Don't worry. I've seen it all." Without waiting for an explicit invitation, Rachel marched past Bill into his living area and studied the layout. "This is actually quite livable. I love the one big room." She glanced down the hallway. "What is this? Two-bed, two-bath?"

"Rachel, why are you here?"

"I sent you two texts, but you never answered. I have intel from last night's bar scene. Plus, I wanted to see your place because I'm considering buying here on the ridge. Since I have an eight-thirty massage on Shamokin Springs Trail, I figured I'd stop by for a chat on the way."

Bill frantically checked his phone. Sure enough. Two messages he'd missed.

"How did you find my place?" he said.

Rachel lifted her hands as if to say it was no great feat. "You're in the directory."

Curly ran two circles around Rachel and Bill, sprinted to his bed, and returned with a stuffed toy.

Rachel stooped to pat Curly's head again. "He's smart. I'd like to get a dog, but I'm always gone."

Bill remained speechless. Given Rachel's beauty and background, he always gave her a wide berth, but now, she was standing in the middle of his home.

"I have to see the balcony, Bill. Is that all right?" Without waiting for an answer, Rachel marched to the sliding door and swung it open.

With hesitation, Bill followed Rachel outside. He glanced to the right and up and was horrified to see Cindy tending winter plants on her balcony.

Oh, jeez.

Bill held his breath, hoping with all his might that Cindy wouldn't notice Rachel Dunn dressed in tight jeans and standing next to him.

But then Rachel thrust her arms wide and half-shouted, "Oh, my word, it's beautiful. It's like you can see the whole world."

"Um, yeah."

Rachel pointed toward Rockfish Valley. "What is that down there? Stoney Creek? I can't see that from my place. You definitely have a better view."

"Yes," said Bill in as soft a voice as he could manage, "it's Stoney Creek."

He glanced right, and his worse fears were confirmed. Cindy was staring at them.

Rachel turned toward Bill and noticed his eyes were drawn to the right. Rachel followed his gaze, saw Cindy, and gave her an enthusiastic wave. "Hey, there! Good morning."

Bill could see Cindy's mouth drop from a distance.

Rachel kept waving.

Cindy managed a tiny wave and said, "Hi."

Rachel turned toward Bill and whispered, "Isn't that Cindy Quintrell?"

"Uh-huh."

Cindy turned and disappeared inside her condo.

"Are you guys like a thing?" said Rachel. "You seemed pretty close when you danced together at the Snow Ball."

Bill continued to stare at Cindy's empty balcony. "A thing? I don't know. We're friends."

"Say, I hope she didn't get the wrong impression. It *is* sort of early. I'd hate for her to assume that I spent the night."

But Rachel wore a half smile. She wasn't concerned about Bill's romantic prospects with Cindy. Life was a game for Rachel Dunn, and she was a skilled player.

"Why did you have to come here?" said Bill. "Why didn't you call?"

"Hey, you've been to my place several times. Uninvited, I might add. You show up with a bunch of questions."

Bill blinked several times. Rachel had a point. Plus, he'd asked her to do him a favor at the Edge the previous night. It wasn't her fault that Cindy had a jealous streak.

"Fair point," he said. "I apologize. Do you want some coffee?"

Rachel nodded. "Yeah. Thanks. I have time for half a cup."

They sat with coffees across the dining table from each other.

"So," said Bill. "What did you learn at the bar?"

Rachel's eyes brightened, and she leaned forward. "You won't believe this."

She had stayed at the bar with Chas Skibinski for several hours.

"It wasn't hard to do," she said. "Chas's eyes told me I could hang around for as long as I wanted."

"Good work," said Bill.

Rachel said that as time passed, the crowd grew louder and louder. Several of Skibinski's employees stopped by to discuss this or that subject. After two drinks, Rachel switched from drinking vodka soda to straight soda to stay fully alert. Later, word spread through the company employees that

Cassandra Key had been shot dead with a high-caliber rifle during a snowstorm. The police had not publicly released those specifics, but Bill wasn't surprised to hear the details had leaked.

That rumor made the rounds for an hour, and then a guy stopped by to put a tidbit in Chas's ear. He said one person had stated a hypothesis about how Key died. The idea spread rapidly, and within minutes, the group reached a consensus.

"Apparently, everyone believed the same thing," said Rachel.

"What's that?" said Bill.

"Cassandra Key was killed by a drone."

TWENTY-SIX

After Rachel left, Bill sat down with a second cup of coffee and considered the drone team's conclusion. From videos of recent warfare, he knew—as did most of the public—that drones were capable of attacking land-based targets with extreme accuracy. But this was the first he'd heard of a drone shooting a person with a rifle. The notion struck him as both plausible and terrifying. And it could potentially explain the accuracy of the shot.

Bill exercised, showered, dressed, and took Curly out for a quick spin around his condo building. Despite the snow on the ground, Curly urged Bill to take him to the slope's edge. Once there, the poodle proudly surveyed the landscape before him. Mountains cascaded from the right down toward the valley. The ridge line across the way resembled a woman lying on her side, wider at the shoulders and hips, narrower at the waist, and simultaneously beautiful and mysterious.

Bill could see his breath. Puffy white clouds floated in an azure sky. The magic of the moment transported Bill's mind far from the investigation. He was simply a retired man out walking his dog.

Suddenly, a drone climbed from below, hovered at Bill's level for an instant, and soared skyward. Bill and Curly both stepped back, surprised by the drone, which now slowly panned the ridge line. Bill turned and pulled on Curly's leash to direct him back to the condo building. With their attention fixed on the ground, Bill and Curly rounded the building's corner toward the front. Then an unknown object flew past them, missing Bill's head by inches. Bill startled, and his heart rate jumped.

What was that?

Bill looked behind him but saw only the snow-covered ground.

Curly growled.

Bill turned back toward the building's front, and a snow-ball smashed against his neck.

Curly barked wildly.

The snowball shattered, and bits of ice made their way under Bill's collar to the skin of his upper chest. Bill searched for his assailant. When another snowball hurtled toward him, Bill dropped Curly's leash and raised his hands to protect his face. Curly raced forward, enraged by the surprise attack.

"Wait," Bill shouted. He ducked the next snowball, began to straighten, and another missile pounded his shoulder.

Ouch.

A darkly clad figure hunkered behind the SUV parked in the first slot.

Curly neared the SUV.

Bill's nostrils flared. Curly was in danger. He hastily formed a snowball and stumbled forward. More icy projectiles hindered his progress, and he was struck again.

Curly disappeared behind the SUV, and his barking ended abruptly.

Oh, no. The assailant has hurt Curly.

Bill sprinted with no regard for his own safety. His assailant ceased firing, perhaps out of ammunition. Heat flushed through Bill. He would tear his assailant apart.

He rounded the SUV with every muscle in his body tense and ready for action.

And there he found Cindy cuddling a joyful Curly.

Bill was speechless.

Though Cindy held Curly with the utmost care, her eyes blazed with anger.

"What in the world has gotten into you?" he demanded.

"Me? What's gotten into me? The better question is, what have you gotten into? Or should I say, *who* have you gotten into?"

Bill's ears grew warm. The snow melted inside his shirt, and a water droplet trickled down his side.

"Well. I mean. Shoot."

"You're not making sense," said Cindy. Her hands gently stroked behind Curly's ears, but a vein in her neck bulged. She clenched her jaw.

Bill said, "You saw Rachel Dunn with me on the balcony."

"Obviously. She appeared absolutely joyful. It must have been quite a night."

"Nothing happened. Rachel came over this morning to see the view."

"Sure. We said no commitments, but there are limits to what I'll consider reasonable behavior. Refresh my memory. Is it true or not that you spent last Tuesday night with me?"

"Technically, no. You asked me to go at two a.m. because you didn't want anyone to see me leaving in the morning."

At this response, Cindy's expression grew even more strained.

"We weren't watching television. Were we?" she said.

"No." Bill considered it unwise to contradict Cindy again. They had, in fact, watched television, but they had also engaged in other activities. He lifted his right hand with his three middle fingers straight up. "Scout's Honor. Nothing happened between Rachel Dunn and me."

"You were never a boy scout."

"It's the sentiment that counts. I promise."

Cindy nodded simply.

Bill got the sudden impression that he had misread the situation.

Cindy's eyes softened, and the muscles in her arms and shoulders relaxed. Her lips quivered with the strain of maintaining a false frown.

"What's going on here?" said Bill.

Cindy burst out laughing.

"You were playing me," he said.

"You should have seen your face."

"Dag nab it. You got my shirt all wet. I should rub your face with snow."

But so great was his relief that he could summon no anger at Cindy's ruse. Instead, he reached to pet Curly on the head.

"So, you never suspected that Rachel and I had . . . you know."

"No, I didn't. Don't take this the wrong way, Bill, but you're no match for Rachel Dunn. She's fifteen years your junior and in fantastic shape." Cindy reached to touch Bill's face. "I'm attracted to you, but we're both older and in average shape. We're a better match, chemistry-wise."

"Otherwise, too, I'd say."

Cindy accompanied him to his building entrance and placed Curly on the sidewalk.

Bill put his hand on Cindy's side, and her arms draped his neck. Her lips were warm and alive.

Curly and Bill watched Cindy stroll to the stairs that led to her building. She turned to give them a parting smile. Curly wagged his tail, and Bill waved.

Warmth spread through Bill's chest. And he entered his condo with renewed determination to find a murderer.

TWENTY-SEVEN

Mitch Gentry slowly cruised the four corners of the shopping center parking lot located off Highway 29 north of Charlottesville. The center had been there a long time—thirty years or so—and provided leased space for an assortment of retail businesses—a grocery store, a liquor store, a mid-size department store, a denture center, a discount variety store, a frame shop, a bakery, and a breakfast restaurant. Mitch examined the buildings and light poles for surveillance cameras but didn't find any. After spending ten minutes touring the property, Mitch parked the squad car to wait for Ritchie Lawrence, his fiancée's cousin.

Mitch and Ritchie had known each other a long time and were good friends. Ritchie was a patrol officer in the Charlottesville Police Department. So when Bill O'Shea suggested Mitch coordinate with Charlottesville, Mitch contacted Ritchie to ask for his advice. Ritchie ran the request through channels and wound up with the assignment of working with Mitch to learn whatever they could about Frank Richardi's activities on the date of the murder. According to the FBI, Richardi had parked his rental car in this lot for four hours.

Ritchie texted that he would be another fifteen minutes. Mitch drove to the breakfast place and bought a medium coffee to go. Leaning on his front bumper outside, he examined the lot's vehicular activity. The property was a large square with a driveway entrance on one side and a one-story, right-angled building on two other sides. Although the parking lot had spaces for several hundred vehicles, less than a third were occupied. Most customers parked close to their retail destinations, leaving the middle of the lot largely empty.

Although Mitch had been to Charlottesville many times, he did not recall shopping in this particular center. That could change soon. His fiancée, Lulu, had been accepted to attend the Virginia Commonwealth University School of Dentistry in Richmond, a two-hour drive from their home in Lyndhurst. A move was in their near future, and a Charlottesville address would give each of them an hour's commute.

The new year promised many changes for Mitch and Lulu. Relocation. Dental school. Wedding. Honeymoon. They were planning a spring wedding, which they had intended to be a small, low-budget affair to save money for dental school. But once they put together a list of family, they realized it would be a large wedding—Mitch and Lulu both had many cousins living in the area, each of whom would be offended if not invited. So they had opted to hold their reception in the church picnic area to minimize expenses. Mitch chuckled at that. No booze helped to keep the cost down, which meant they could spend more on the honeymoon. Mitch smiled. The honeymoon planning was his job, and he had his sights on an all-inclusive resort in the Caribbean. Blue sky. White sand beaches. Rum punch.

So lost was Mitch in his daydream that he didn't notice Ritchie's cruiser until it pulled up next to him.

"What's up?" said Ritchie, after he had exited the car and shaken Mitch's hand.

"I have a Caribbean honeymoon dancing in my head."

Ritchie grinned and nodded. He stood six foot three with long arms and big hands. Mitch and Ritchie had played high school football together—Mitch as a linebacker and Ritchie as a wide receiver. Ritchie had dark brown skin, short hair, and a big smile that rarely left his face.

"How do you figure we should approach this?" said Mitch.

They conferred and decided to work on each business as a team.

"Shall we start with the breakfast restaurant?" said Ritchie.

"Sounds good."

The manager at Bonnie's Breakfast Place—a woman named Sharone—was on duty and happy to help. The three met briefly in Sharone's tiny office in a back corner of the kitchen. Yes, they had video surveillance of the entryways and nearby parking spaces. She could show Ritchie how to scan the digital recording for the morning of the murder, and Mitch could interview individual workers at a two-top table in the dining room.

Mitch met first with a cook named Theo, who appeared to be in his late forties to early fifties.

Mitch explained the reason they were there.

"A murder investigation!" said Theo, and his eyes widened.

"That's right," said Mitch. He showed Theo a printed photograph of Richardi's silver Avalon. "We believe this car was parked at the shopping center for four hours on Friday morning. Did you happen to see it?"

Perhaps as a courtesy, Theo examined the photo carefully,

but then he frowned. "I'm too busy cooking to notice what's going on outside. On my breaks, I go out the back to grab a quick smoke and don't see the parking lot."

"Okay. Thanks."

Mitch interviewed the eight on-duty employees with similar results. Ritchie scanned five hours of video at high speed without seeing a single Avalon. Two employees who had worked the morning of the murder were not currently on duty, and Sharone promised to share a digital copy of the Avalon photo with them.

In a similar fashion, Mitch and Ritchie tackled the frame shop, the liquor store, and the denture center. Some employees had come through the parking lot at the right time but not noticed an Avalon. The frame shop and denture center had no video surveillance. The liquor store video only captured the store, the sidewalk outside, and a few of the nearby parking spaces. The grocery store had many more employees, and they spent ninety minutes working with the assistant manager to rotate employees into a back room for quick interviews.

Then they decided to break for lunch.

Outside the grocery store, Ritchie stretched his arms high above his head and examined the massive shopping center parking lot.

"There must be three hundred spaces out there," he said.

"Yep. It would be helpful if the center had video surveillance of the whole lot."

Ritchie twisted his lips into a bunch. "Maybe, but on the other hand, I don't like the feeling that I'm always being watched."

"I know what you mean. We've got a drone show coming up in Wintergreen. The company conducts practice flights, and it seems like there's always one overhead."

Ritchie grimaced. "Jeez. That's creepy."

"We'd better get used to it," said Mitch.

"What do you mean? Once the show's over, they'll all leave. Right?"

"Sure. But manufacturers are making more drones all the time. In the future, they'll be everywhere."

TWENTY-EIGHT

B ill had arranged to meet Tanya Stafford at the Highlands condos at twelve thirty. After the snowball fight with Cindy, Bill spent more time researching drones on his laptop. Then, he grew hungry and walked to the small cafe on Blue Ridge Drive for an early lunch. When Bill opened the door to Café Devine, the bell that hung from the doorknob jingled. Kim Wiley, the proprietor, stood behind the counter having a quiet conversation with a woman he didn't recognize. There were no other customers in the store, and at the sound of the bell, both women glanced his way.

"As I live and breathe, it's Bill O'Shea," exclaimed Kim. "It's been so long since you stopped in, I thought you died and I missed the funeral."

"Don't start that, Kim," he said. "I bought wine here last Thursday. A Malbec, as I recall. You recommended it."

Kim put her hands on her hips and said, "I don't remember that." Her hair was brown, frizzy, and unmanageable. She wore it cut in a medium length that didn't quite reach her shoulders. Without another word, Kim returned to the other woman, who glanced nervously at Bill. Kim took several steps to her right, away from Bill, and the woman followed. They resumed their conversation in low voices.

Bill leaned over to inspect the display case of freshly made lunch choices. The egg salad called to him. His stomach grumbled. After selecting flavored sparkling water from the beverage fridge, he stepped to the cash register and waited for Kim to return. Kim's nephew Nathan prepared food in the small kitchen behind the counter. Nathan noticed Bill waiting and reached for a towel to wipe his hands, but then Kim and the other woman exchanged goodbyes, and Kim returned to the register.

Kim leaned toward Bill and said, "I gather you're helping Emily investigate Cassandra Key's murder."

"Who told you that?"

"Does it matter? The word's all over the mountain."

Kim's avocation was brokering gossip among mountain residents. Try as he might, Bill had never convinced Kim to reveal a source, and he now believed he never would.

"Have you solved the case yet?" she asked.

"You know I can't discuss specifics."

"I hope you guys solve it soon. A random murder tends to make people nervous. The woman who was just in here? She told me they're considering leaving Wintergreen until the police catch the killer."

"That hardly seems necessary. I *can* tell you this much. This was not a random murder."

"Good to know," said Kim, and she took Bill's order for an egg salad sandwich and chips. After relaying the order to Nathan, Kim stood back from the counter with her arms crossed. Her eyes twinkled, and her lips turned up in a smile. Bill recognized that expression.

"Do you know something I should know?" he said.

"Maybe."

"Go ahead now. Spill it. Justice is impatient."

Kim turned toward Nathan and said, "Bill and I are going to grab a chat. Will you mind the register, please?"

"Yes, ma'am."

Kim came from behind the counter and led Bill to one of several small tables. Once seated, she put her arms on the table and spoke in a low voice. "When I heard that the victim was here for an executive retreat, I searched for her name and discovered she was president of the Old Virginia Gun Club."

"Very resourceful."

"Thank you. The club's website includes Cassandra Key's bio with a photo, and I recognized her immediately."

"Wait. How do you know Ms. Key?"

"I'll get to that in a minute."

Nathan approached with Bill's sandwich and chips, and Kim paused long enough for Nathan to leave the food and return to the kitchen.

"Out of curiosity, I studied the photos of the other club executives, figuring they might be here for the retreat as well. Sure enough, the man named Kent Olsen stopped here last night with a dark-haired woman to purchase a bottle of wine. By their body language, I ascertained they were a couple. Then I noticed she was wearing a large sapphire engagement ring. From our chitchat, I learned they were staying in the Highlands condos."

"Goodness, Kim. You should apply for a detective's license."

Kim tilted her head as if giving consideration to Bill's suggestion. "No, I like running a cafe too much."

Bill chewed the inside of his cheek, impatient to hear the gossip Kim considered relevant to the case. But he didn't try to hurry her, because Kim only revealed secrets in her own time.

"You know my sister, Jessica, lives in Staunton," said Kim.

"I did not know that, but thanks for sharing."

"Anyway, I visited her the night before Ms. Key's murder. We dined at the Mill Street Grill. It's a tradition of ours. We dine out once a month and always pick a local restaurant in Staunton."

"Okay. How is that relevant to my investigation?"

Kim raised her eyebrows. "I saw Cassandra Key at the restaurant."

Bill leaned forward.

"It was quite a spectacle," said Kim.

"What's that?"

"The way the couple next to us was carrying on. They were sitting on the same side of the booth with their hands all over each other. It was get-a-room time. Know what I mean?"

Bill nodded.

"I wouldn't have noticed them except for their behavior. As it was, I could hardly keep my eyes away. And that's how I remembered Ms. Key."

Bill leaned forward. "Excuse me. You witnessed Cassandra Key with a man the night before her death?"

Kim smiled proudly. "Yes, indeed. And guess who the man was. That's right—no other than the man who visited my cafe with his fiancée last night. Kent Olsen."

To confirm, Bill said, "Cassandra Key and Kent Olsen had dinner in Staunton, and they were groping each other. You're sure about this?"

Kim paused to reflect. "Yes. Groping. That's the right word for it."

Bill eyed his untouched egg salad sandwich. He took a large bite but hardly noticed the delicious blend of flavors. Instead, his mind grappled with Kim's revelation. Kent Olsen had had an affair with Cassandra Key years earlier, but according to Nikki Churchill, the relationship ended amicably. The parties had purportedly moved on. Apparently not.

"And I saw them again when Jessica and I left the restaurant," said Kim. "They were having an animated conversation in the parking lot."

"Did you hear what they said?"

"Just a few words when we passed by their car. Kent said, 'I'm serious. This has to end.' Then Cassandra said, 'It's up to you. It's totally your call.' That's all I heard except for her laugh. She laughed again and again. It was a taunting laugh I'll never forget. And the fury on Olsen's face under the streetlight. I won't forget that either."

TWENTY-NINE

Mitch and Ritchie Lawrence ate at a nearby Chick-fil-A. Mitch ordered the grilled chicken sandwich with waffle fries, a side order of coleslaw, and lemonade. Ritchie ordered a similar meal but opted for the breaded filet.

"Why do you get the grilled chicken?" Ritchie asked after they were seated at a window table. "The breaded tastes better."

"Lulu convinced me to try it. She claims the grilled is better for your health. Now I've grown to like it."

Ritchie pointed at Mitch. "See? That's the problem with women right there. They change you, little by little."

"I don't mind," said Mitch.

"That's because you're a man and in love. You don't even notice it's happening. It's the tiny behavioral tweaks. The brand of paper towels you use. The dishes that can and cannot go in the dishwasher. Whether you sleep with the windows open or closed."

Mitch frowned because it occurred to him that there might be some truth in what Ritchie said. Before moving in with Lulu, he had never bothered much with tissues. Now there was a box of tissues in every room except the garage. And if they ran out of tissues in one room and there were no extras in the closet, it constituted a national crisis.

"I'm telling you," said Ritchie. "One day, you'll wake up and realize you still resemble you, but you behave exactly like her. Pay attention to this stuff."

Mitch took a mental note to do as Ritchie had suggested, but he didn't say anything. He would not bad-mouth Lulu in front of her cousin. If he did, like as not, word would get back to Lulu before the day was over. No, Mitch was smarter than that.

The two men ate in silence for a few minutes, and then Ritchie asked Mitch what was going on with Lulu and dental school. Mitch shared that she would begin classes at VCU soon, and they would move to Charlottesville to split their commute between Wintergreen and Richmond.

Another minute passed by, then Ritchie said, "If you're going to live here, you might as well apply for a job with the Charlottesville PD."

"Nah. I'm good. I like working in Wintergreen."

"We have a lot of openings and a much bigger budget. You'd probably get a raise."

Hmm. With Lulu quitting work to study full-time, they would be short of money for a few years. So a raise would definitely help. And there was another consideration. Mitch had begun his law enforcement career as a cop in Richmond and then joined the Wintergreen Police Department to be closer to Lulu. Though he enjoyed his work as a patrol officer, he aspired to eventually become a full-fledged detective. Unfortunately, given the size of Wintergreen's police force, there were few opportunities for advancement. Then there was the commute time—Charlottesville to Wintergreen was an hour's drive.

"I'll put in a word if you want," said Ritchie. "I'm sure my boss would like to meet you."

"I don't know."

"Take an interview. That doesn't cost you anything."

"Yeah. Maybe I should."

After lunch, Mitch and Ritchie returned to canvassing the shopping center's retail businesses. They worked the fabric store, the bakery, a smoke shop, and the mid-size department store, which took over an hour on its own. By then, it was mid-afternoon, and they had little to show for their time.

Standing next to their squad cars, Ritchie said, "Looks like a bust."

"I'm not too surprised," said Mitch. "I don't take notice of a randomly parked car unless there's something different about it." He was disappointed to have wasted an entire day, but Mitch supposed that detective work often involved a lot of digging to find a single clue.

Ritchie's phone buzzed. He glanced at the screen and pushed his lips out. "Huh. It's Sharone, the manager from the breakfast place."

"This is Officer Lawrence," he said, with his phone to his ear. "Hey, Sharone. What's up?" He listened a few moments. "Oh, yeah? That's terrific. We'll be right over."

After the breakfast rush faded, Sharone had called the off-duty employees who had worked the morning of Key's death. One of them remembered seeing a silver Avalon. Sharone had asked the employee to come in, and she would be there in ten minutes.

On the drive across the parking lot, Mitch took slow, deep breaths to settle his nerves.

DeeAnn arrived a few minutes later, and Sharone brought her to where Mitch and Ritchie were standing. In an old winter coat, a cute sweater, and jeans, DeeAnn was in her mid-thirties and had shiny blond hair and blue eyes. She was a bit overweight, and the skin of her neck appeared loose for a woman of her age.

Sharone introduced them, then added, "I should have thought of DeeAnn's exercise routine when we spoke earlier. She was more likely than anyone to notice the car."

"How's that?" said Ritchie.

"On days when DeeAnn works a double, she spends most of her meal break hiking the perimeter of the lot."

DeeAnn nodded. "Three times around is twenty-five hundred steps."

Sharone put her hand on DeeAnn's shoulder as if DeeAnn was a sister or a close friend. "It's all part of her program. Tell them, DeeAnn."

DeeAnn nodded again. "I'm on the PC&E diet."

"PC&E?" said Mitch. "I'm not familiar with that one. What's it about?"

"Oh, okay." DeeAnn stood with her hands together in front. She nervously squeezed the fingers of her left hand. "PC&E stands for portion control and exercise. I can eat and drink everything I used to, but not as much. I track my calories and never go over two thousand. On the exercise side, I walk a lot, like five miles every day."

Sharone's face lit up. "DeeAnn has lost thirty pounds in the last year."

A tinge of pink crept onto DeeAnn's face. "It's going good so far. My goal is to lose another twenty pounds."

"That's impressive," said Ritchie.

"All right," said Sharone. "You three can take that booth over there. Want some water or coffee or something?"

They all asked for water, and Sharone left to fetch them.

Mitch and Ritchie squeezed into one side of the booth, and DeeAnn took the other. Mitch explained why he and

Ritchie had spent the day in the shopping center. When he mentioned the words murder investigation, DeeAnn took a quick breath.

Ritchie gave her a warm smile and passed the photo they had across the table. "Sharone mentioned that you might have seen a vehicle like this in the parking lot Friday morning."

"Yes," said DeeAnn, "that's it. A Toyota Avalon. I drive an Avalon myself, although mine is fifteen years old. This one is much newer."

"What time was this?" said Ritchie.

"About eight forty. My shift started at four thirty, so yeah, eight forty."

DeeAnn said she first noticed the Avalon because it was parked by itself in the middle of the lot. Then she saw that the driver—still seated in the car—had kept the engine running, which made her nervous.

"I've always been told you shouldn't sit in an idling car for more than a minute because it's not good for your health. I don't know if it's true or not, but that's what I've been told."

Mitch gave DeeAnn a nod of encouragement. "It's a smart rule of thumb."

After keeping an eye on the Avalon for an entire loop around the lot—which took her eight minutes—DeeAnn decided if the car was still idling at the end of her workout, she would approach the vehicle and invite the driver to wait inside the restaurant.

She's a nice person, Mitch thought. *You don't meet those every day.*

"So, when I came to the bakery on my third loop, I started to cut across the parking lot, but I had only taken a few steps when a full-size pickup hauling a trailer drove up and parked between the Avalon and me. The truck and trailer took up two parking spaces and then some, which made me mad because

I'd have to circle around them to get to the Avalon. I stopped and went back to the sidewalk to see if the truck would move on."

Ritchie put his forearms on the table and leaned forward.

DeeAnn said, "But it didn't. A few moments later, the truck driver got out and walked straight here to Bonnie's. I edged down a bit to check on the Avalon and was surprised to see that the driver had gotten out of his car. And here's the funny thing. That driver got into the pickup and hauled the trailer away."

Mitch's heart rate picked up speed. Art Rossi had reported seeing a truck and trailer parked at the end of Old Stoney Creek Road.

"Can you describe the pickup?" he said.

"White. It might have been an F-150. The trailer carried something that was covered with a green tarp."

Ritchie opened his phone to take notes. "Do you remember what the men looked like?"

DeeAnn nodded. "They were both white. The driver of the truck was average height, and he wore a dark jacket. I saw him later when I came inside the restaurant. He had brown hair and a thick mustache."

"And the driver of the Avalon?" said Ritchie.

"I didn't see him up close. He was tall and had a lot of gray in his hair."

"How big was the cargo on the trailer?" asked Mitch.

DeeAnn tilted her head back to think it over. "Not huge. About the size of a big riding lawn mower."

Mitch and Ritchie exchanged glances. If the truck left the shopping center at eight forty, Frank Richardi could have reached Nellysford by nine thirty. Art Rossi had reported seeing an F-150 with an empty flatbed trailer at ten forty-five.

"When I went back inside to finish my double," said

DeeAnn, "I checked for the driver of the truck because I was curious. He was seated in another section. Then I got back to work. When I came out of the restaurant at two thirty, I searched for the Avalon, but it was gone."

Which made sense because, by two thirty, the former FBI analyst had spotted Frank Richardi in Warrenton.

"I hope this is helpful," said DeeAnn.

Mitch and Ritchie assured DeeAnn it was and thanked her for coming in on her day off. After exchanging quick good-byes with Sharone, the two officers stepped outside and conferred next to Mitch's cruiser.

"What do you make of that?" said Ritchie.

"It's important," said Mitch. "I need to call it into the chief. Appreciate you helping out."

"How about joining the Charlottesville PD? Do you want to meet with my boss?"

Mitch hesitated. "Maybe. Let me think it over some more."

THIRTY

Bill met Tanya Stafford in the parking lot of the Highlands condominium complex. Tree branches danced in the harsh wind. The blue skies had vanished with the onset of cloud reinforcements, and the temperature had fallen into the twenties. Bill zipped his coat as high as it would go.

At the parking lot, Bill approached Tanya standing next to her car.

Tanya bounced on her toes and rubbed her hands up and down her arms. "Gosh, it's chilly out here."

"Sure is. Thanks for coming. This shouldn't take long."

Tanya nodded, and Bill escorted her to the building entrance that led to Olsen's rented condo. On his earlier visit, Bill had noticed the hallway on Olsen's floor contained a large back window that provided nearly the same vantage point as Olsen's balcony. Although Bill didn't wish to encounter Olsen right then, the benefit of getting Tanya's assessment outweighed that risk.

From where they stood at the window, Bill and Tanya could see the upper chairlift station and the Wild Turkey ski run. Resort operations had reopened the Highlands area, and the chairlift was running. The lift station motor hummed loudly as it hauled its human cargo up the mountain.

A third of the way down the Wild Turkey run, an orange barrel on the left marked where Loggers Alley Trail crossed the ski run. Cassandra Key was shot when standing on Loggers Alley underneath the chairlift. Bill oriented Tanya to the setting.

"Goodness," she said, "that must be four hundred yards. Where was the shooter?"

"We don't know," said Bill. "Theoretically, they could have taken the shot from any of these balconies. Or from a position in the woods. One of the suspects is staying in this unit here." He pointed to Olsen's balcony, which jutted out from the building a few feet to their left.

"What were the conditions?" asked Tanya. "It stormed that day, right?"

Bill explained that the shooting occurred as the storm's front edge hit Wintergreen. Winds were high, the snow was intermittent, and low-hanging clouds drifted across the mountain. Forensic analysis determined that Key had been shot twice in the chest within the span of one second and that she had died quickly from blood loss. Also, a morning walker reported hearing two rifle shots.

Vertical lines formed on Tanya's forehead. Her eyes narrowed. She cupped her hands around her eyes to focus on the target zone. After studying the shot, Tanya faced Bill and shook her head.

"I couldn't make that shot. Not in the middle of a snowstorm. On a clear day, sure, I could probably hit a target from this distance. But with poor visibility? And high winds?"

"What about Bryan McCasland?"

Tanya frowned mightily. "I doubt it."

"Assume for a moment that McCasland did make the shot. Could he have shot her again one second later?"

Tanya scrunched her nose. "No way. When firing at a long-range target, I take at least a few seconds to readjust my sight picture and re-sync my breathing. Firing two accurate shots in one second in the middle of a storm? That strikes me as impossible."

At that moment, a drone flew into view from behind them, shot out a hundred yards, and began a slow descent along the ridge to their left. Bill guessed it was one of the marketing flights Skibinski had mentioned earlier. The drone would capture a stunning view of the ridge condos.

Tanya had apparently not noticed. Her eyes remained fixed on the location of Cassandra Key's death. Tanya shook her head again. "No, Bill, I don't see how anyone could make two shots like that in one second. I'm amazed. It's as if the shots were fired by a machine."

THIRTY-ONE

B ill had arranged to meet Mitch in Rockfish Valley at the top of Old Stoney Creek Road. From Route 151, Bill turned left on a two-lane road that wound gently past single-family homesites carved out of a hardwood forest. After a mile, the small stream named Stoney Creek crept into view on the right. At the end of the road on the left, there was a small white house with a dark roof. A dirt pathway wide enough for one car extended onward to the right. Bill drove another fifty yards and parked behind Mitch's cruiser in front of a closed yellow gate.

The temperature gauge on the Mazda's dash had climbed into the thirties on the way down from Wintergreen. Generally, the valley was ten to twelve degrees warmer, but it was still cold enough that the two of them sat in the squad car with the heater running.

Mitch unfolded the Wintergreen trail map and pointed to an inset depicting the Lower Shamokin Falls Trail.

"Okay, so we're right here. The trail begins on the other side of that gate and goes a mile and half before reaching the falls."

"How far is that from the crime scene?"

Mitch shrugged. "Not sure. There are twists and turns. If we could travel in a straight line, I'd guess we're less than two miles from where Ms. Key was shot."

Bill had never hiked the Lower Shamokin Falls Trail and didn't feel a need to go the full distance now. But Art Rossi had reported seeing a truck and trailer parked at the gate. After hiking to the power substation, Art had grown spooked enough to turn around.

Bill said, "Let's go up to the substation and see what we see."

Bill and Mitch walked around the gate and began a gradual ascent along a jeep road. After a few minutes, the substation came into view on the left. A small building, which Bill guessed was the pump station, lay straight ahead. The jeep road cut right at the pump station and crossed Stoney Creek. Before the creek, a little sign pointed the way to a pedestrian bridge behind the pump station. They paused at the middle of the bridge and gazed upstream. Much of the snow Art Rossi had seen in the trees had melted. The stream gurgled below them.

Bill imagined Frank Richardi standing on the trail beyond the bridge, fiddling with a drone controller. Richardi heard something and spotted Art Rossi approaching. Then, Richardi had hidden somewhere, perhaps behind a tree or a boulder. Art reached the bridge, paused to observe the view, and then got spooked. Maybe Art subconsciously detected something —the sound of Richardi's breathing or his fingers tapping on the keys. Whatever sensory data triggered Art's fear, the decision to turn around had likely saved his life.

"One thing is bothering me," said Mitch. "Ms. Key was shot from the front while facing uphill. If Frank Richardi used this trail to reach her, he would have had to hike above her to take the shot. That seems like a stupid plan. Why didn't he just drive to Wintergreen? And what's with the trailer?"

Bill said, "The problem with going to Wintergreen was the community had only one road out. If someone had seen Key getting shot, the police might have blocked the road before Richardi made his escape. But that doesn't matter anyway, because Richardi didn't have to hike to a point above Cassandra Key."

"No? Why not?"

"Because he pulled the trigger from here."

THIRTY-TWO

C has Skibinski agreed to meet Bill on short notice under the condition that Bill joined him in Nellysford. The resort wanted aerial footage of the Stoney Creek community for promotional purposes, and Chas had chosen to film that segment himself. Bill met him in the open field used for farmer's market days in the mild weather months. The valley's warmer temperatures had melted much of the snow, and the ground was colored a mix of brown and white.

After brief greetings, Chas launched his drone. The machine hovered near them a few moments, and then Chas sent it skyward several hundred feet. The drone was now a speck, and the propellers' noise faded into the background.

The controller Chas used to direct the drone fit easily in his hands, and the screen displayed the camera view with remarkable precision. First, Chas zoomed out the camera until the display captured all of Stoney Creek, Nellysford, and the surrounding countryside. Then he made an adjustment, and the view zoomed in to capture the top of Bill's head.

Bill turned his gaze skyward, expecting to see the drone

immediately above him, but it was still several hundred feet high.

"Amazing," said Bill.

"Watch this."

Chas directed the drone to the nearby highway—Route 151—where it hovered forty feet from the ground near the Stoney Creek community entrance. A mid-size SUV coming from the neighborhood turned right on 151. After the SUV made the turn, Chas brought the drone to a position behind the vehicle and had the drone follow it through town.

"Is that legal?" said Bill. "Tailing someone like that?"

"Technically, I'm in compliance provided I don't hover over their car, but I'm not supposed to follow them like this, so I'll peel off even though they don't know I'm there."

Chas then explained that pilots were allowed to fly drones in public airspace below four hundred feet unless restricted by regulations like the Wintergreen policy.

Bill was grateful for the policy. He had not moved far from the city only to find the sky filled with remotely piloted aircraft.

"Want to fly it?" asked Skibinski.

Bill drew his head back. "I've never flown a drone."

"It's not hard. Let me show you."

"I don't want to crash it."

"I won't let you crash."

Bill had flown in private, single-engine airplanes several times but never been offered the controls. Truthfully, he was happy leaving the flying to others, but this was different. The drone was no larger than a backpack, and Bill was standing safely on the ground. Bill accepted Skibinski's invitation, and after receiving two minutes of instruction, he took the controls with nervous hands.

Chas had pulled the drone to a height of several hundred

feet, and Bill kept it flying in one position until his heart began to settle. Then he brought the drone back to the entrance of Stoney Creek and followed the road into the neighborhood. They passed a golf fairway on the right and the clubhouse on the left. Then they cruised by the tennis courts and the resort swimming pool. At the intersection with Stoney Creek West, Bill turned left and floated above private homes in the area. The snow-covered hills took his breath away. A wisp of smoke rose from a chimney. Bill zoomed in on a man splitting wood in his backyard.

Wow! This is fun.

He flew Skibinski's drone for a few minutes and then handed back the controls. After thanking Chas, Bill asked about the drone's range.

"It varies from one machine to the next. For example, this drone has a maximum operating distance of nine miles, but it's a higher-end model."

Bill said he had a few follow-up questions from their previous conversation.

"Ask away," said Chas, his eyes still on the controls. "I can multitask."

Bill shared that Rachel had overheard someone at the bar say they believed Cassandra Key was killed by a drone. Did Chas share that view?

"Yes," said Chas, "it's possible. I didn't know the specifics of how she was killed when we last spoke. If I had, the notion might have occurred to me then."

"So, how would that work?"

Chas explained that militaries worldwide were in a race to improve their fighting capability by acquiring the latest drone technology. Several high-tech weapons providers had announced plans to sell remotely operated drones equipped with infantry weapons—sniper rifles and machine guns. The smart weapons used sophisticated computer vision technology and tracking algorithms capable of hitting static or moving targets in the daytime or at night.

"Does the accuracy change during a cloud cover?"

"No. It's the same principle. Once the target has been sighted, thermal imaging technology can track it. Of course, the drone would have to weather the precipitation, low temperatures, and high winds we had that day. But I'm sure weapons designers have sorted all that out."

"And the drone could hit a moving target?"

"Yes. Assuming the drone was equipped with the right sensory equipment and tracking software."

What a horrifying scenario. The arms race was alive and well. If militaries had drones equipped with sniper rifles, how long would it take the bad guys to acquire them? Bill generally dismissed the sentiments of people who pined for the good old days, but maybe they were right. Maybe the best times were in the past.

Bill thanked Chas for his insight into the latest drone capabilities but then made what promised to be a controversial statement. "I believe one of your drone operators enabled this murder."

Chas tore his eyes from the drone display and glared at Bill. "Why would you say that?"

"We never see drones in Wintergreen. It would be an incredible coincidence for a drone-enabled murder to occur in the same week your drones are flying around. The two events must be connected somehow. You have to admit that one of your pilots might be involved."

Chas hit the Return Home button and turned toward Bill. "Why would one of my employees care about Cassandra Key?"

"I don't know. Maybe your pilot didn't kill Key. Maybe they just supplied the drone."

Chas turned his eyes skyward and watched his drone slowly settle to the ground. He took a deep breath and said, "It's possible. I don't have full-time positions for drone pilots, and I don't know all of them well. They do other stuff to make ends meet. Some work for other drone companies. Some work for manufacturers or have their own small businesses that rely on drone technology. But with the Key murder, you're talking about a military application. You can't buy that kind of stuff on the internet."

"Okay. Say I wanted to buy such a drone. How would I go about it?"

Skibinski lifted his hands as if the answer was obvious. "Contact an arms dealer. Look for someone with military connections. I stay away from the arms race. It's not my thing."

"But it's possible that one of your part-time drone pilots could supply a sniper-enabled drone for the right price. Isn't it?"

Skibinski rubbed his chin. "Maybe. One of them might have a connection to the arms world. And one or two have the technical skills to build a killer drone in their garage."

"Good. Good. Give me some names."

Chas Skibinski said he needed time. He didn't have the names on hand and didn't want his pilots to think he was working for the police. He'd have to ask a few questions, and he must tread lightly.

On Bill's return drive up the mountain, he kept his eyes on the road, but his mind was wrestling with something Chas had said.

Look for someone with military connections.

THIRTY-THREE

After the initial flood of reports Krista received of unusual activity in the Highlands Express area, new leads had slowed to a trickle. With Bill interviewing interested parties and Mitch working the FBI lead down in Charlottesville, Krista had begun to feel left out, so she was pleased when Emily asked her to join the investigation update.

Four people sat around the conference room table—Emily, Bill, Mitch, and Krista. Nelson County's Undersheriff Arnie Shields joined via video. Mitch, Bill, and Krista took turns reporting what they had learned in the last twenty-four hours, and then the five of them went back and forth a while. Arnie Shields expressed great skepticism regarding Bill's theory that a professional killer had used a drone to shoot Cassandra Key.

"I get it," said Bill. "It sounds incredible, but the expert I consulted doesn't believe a human could hit a target from that distance in a snowstorm. Certainly not twice in one second."

"We only have one witness on the timing of the shots," said Arnie. "Perhaps he had it wrong."

But Emily said, "No, Arnie, Soren Larsen confirmed the timing. He said the two shots had to come close together for the bullets to enter the victim's body the way they did."

Arnie frowned. "Okay. I'm warming up to the drone thing. Now, can someone summarize where we are?"

Emily held out a hand to indicate Bill should take the lead.

Bill scratched his head. "Okay, we have a lot of moving parts here."

In the next few minutes, Bill gave his summary. Cassandra Key had assembled the Old Virginia Gun Club trustees for an executive retreat in Wintergreen at the same time a drone company was preparing for a nighttime show. Someone hired Frank Richardi out of retirement to murder Cassandra Key, and Richardi chose to use the latest drone technology as his weapon of choice.

"Why would he do that?" asked Arnie. "Why not shoot her in a parking lot?"

"I don't know," said Bill. "Perhaps he believed a drone killing would be harder for us to solve. There's some truth in that. If the FBI hadn't spotted Frank Richardi in Warrenton and Art Rossi had not seen the parked trailer on Old Stoney Creek Road, we would have never put it together."

"I still haven't put it together," said Arnie. "But please, continue."

Bill said, "Frank Richardi flew in from Martinique and picked up the drone in the Charlottesville parking lot. He then drove to Nellysford and parked on Old Stoney Creek Road, where he launched the drone. Flying in a straight line, it's less than two miles from that point to where Key was shot. This is well within the operational distance of military-style drones.

"Hiding in the woods below, Richardi operated the drone using a remote control. The drone used smart technology to sight the target and fire its mounted rifle. Once the deed was done, Richardi drove back to Charlottesville, retrieved his rental car, and was subsequently spotted by the FBI in Warrenton." Bill paused to glance at Arnie on the video screen, then said, "At this point, I have to venture into speculative territory."

"Don't let that stop you," said Arnie.

Bill didn't. "Richardi is not the murderer. He's the weapon. Someone else hired Richardi, and they might have also helped Richardi conduct the hit by identifying Key on the hiking trail. Kent Olsen and Elsie Dale have an unobstructed view from their balcony to the site where Cassandra was shot. Bryan McCasland is staying in a nearby condo."

Krista eyed the others in the meeting. Everyone seemed to be following Bill. Fine. They had a plausible means sorted out. But as far as she could tell, they still had several open questions.

"Who delivered the trailer to Richardi?" said Emily.

"We don't know," said Bill. "But it's possible the supplier is somehow connected to this drone show. So I put pressure on Skibinski to give me a name."

"Is that person the money?" said Arnie.

"Perhaps," said Bill, "but not necessarily." Bill explained that he believed the person behind the murder was close to Cassandra Key and may or may not have come to the board's executive retreat.

"By the way," he said. "Have we tracked down the fourth director, Allen Steele?"

Finally, thought Krista, *a question I can answer.*

"Not yet," she said. "I've called Steele's daughter multiple times without success. Now, her voice mailbox is full."

Emily frowned, then summarized her understanding of where they stood. "Okay. It appears that Richardi's identity remains our best clue. If we can find a connection between Richardi and someone close to Cassandra Key, we'll have our murderer."

Bill nodded and said, "I've got a call with my FBI contact in an hour. Hopefully, he's got the full scoop on Richardi."

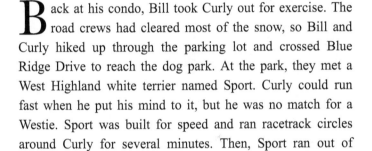

Back at his condo, Bill took Curly out for exercise. The road crews had cleared most of the snow, so Bill and Curly hiked up through the parking lot and crossed Blue Ridge Drive to reach the dog park. At the park, they met a West Highland white terrier named Sport. Curly could run fast when he put his mind to it, but he was no match for a Westie. Sport was built for speed and ran racetrack circles around Curly for several minutes. Then, Sport ran out of steam and lay on his side with his tongue hanging out. Sport's owner, a tall man with gray hair, let the Westie rest a few minutes, then scooped him up and headed toward their home in the other direction.

Bill sat on the picnic table and let Curly wander as he would. After a few minutes, they would have to go home so Bill could get ready for his dinner with Wanda and Amy. But before leaving the park, his phone buzzed. Skip Forrester.

"This guy Richardi has quite the file," said Skip. "I've been through most of it. The FBI has been aware of his existence for decades. We got close to him twice but could never make a case that would stick. We even tried offering him a deal. No luck. Then he disappeared."

"What can you tell me about him?"

"Strange guy. Very innovative for his profession. The FBI has a nickname for him—the Edison of killers. Lots of these guys stick to the same MO—like a carpenter with a hammer. Not Frank Richardi. He custom-designed tactics to match each job and was known to wait years before executing his hits. As a result, he was darn hard to catch. The team is certain he once killed a corporate snitch by inducing cardiac arrest, but several coroners could not agree on whether the man died of natural causes or was murdered."

Skip added that the FBI believed Richardi had close ties to organized crime in the US. However, he had also dabbled in international work and done a few corporate hits. Bill asked if Skip would put together a summary of Richardi's known clients. If so, Wintergreen would search for a connection between a client and Cassandra Key. Skip agreed to pull the data and then asked what Wintergreen had learned that day.

"Wait a minute," Skip said, after Bill's summary. "You believe Richardi used a smart drone to kill Ms. Key?"

"Looks that way."

"That puts this investigation in a new light," said Skip. "News that a smart drone killed a civilian will spread through the FBI faster than a rumor of budget cuts."

Skip explained that this kind of technology was only available in the military space. The FBI was concerned that if the technology fell into the wrong hands—drug cartels and terrorists—violent crime would become harder to prevent and detect. Once in a great while, military weapons went missing and wound up in the wrong hands. Smart weapons had not yet made their way from military supplies to the black market, but some feared it was only a matter of time. A special task force had been assembled to investigate, and Skip was on that task force.

"That's interesting," said Bill.

A vast understatement, Skip claimed. Skip apparently took his task force duties seriously because he ended the call with a brief statement of intent.

"I'm coming to Wintergreen."

THIRTY-FOUR

B ill returned home from the dog park to shower and change into slacks and a sweater. After pulling on a jacket, he walked through his parking lot to Blue Ridge Drive. Directly across the street from Bill's condo, a driveway led to the tennis center, the golf course pro shop, and the Devils Grill restaurant. Bill had made a seven o'clock reservation for three and arrived ten minutes early.

The Devils Grill was a comfortable place with soft lighting, carpeted floors, and dark wooden beams running across the ceiling. Given its convenient location to his condo, Bill was a regular customer. He checked in with the hostess and moseyed to the bar, where a hockey game was in progress on a flat-screen television. While he waited, the bartender brought him a glass of ice water.

A few minutes later, Wanda entered the restaurant alone, and Bill's heartbeat quickened. Even after five years of divorce, his eyes naturally gravitated toward her. She wore jeans with boots, a light-brown turtleneck sweater, and a long, dark coat. He hurried to her side at the hostess's station.

"Where's Amy?" he said after Wanda gave him a hug.

"She's having takeout at the condo. Claimed she was tired."

"Oh. I'm sorry."

"It's all right. We can talk about stuff we wouldn't if Amy were here." Wanda's eyes smiled mischievously.

Bill followed Wanda and the hostess toward a table on the left side of the room and wondered what stuff they needed to discuss. Wanda walked briskly. Her auburn hair hung carelessly atop her coat collar.

The hostess placed their menus at a table for four. Wanda sat with her back to the wall, and Bill hesitated, unsure whether he should sit beside her or across the table.

Wanda must have guessed he was debating the issue because she said, "Lord, Bill, sit next to me. I won't bite."

He laughed nervously, sat, and scanned the room for familiar faces. His Wintergreen friends knew that he and Cindy were close, and word traveled fast on the mountain. Anyone who saw him out with Wanda and Amy would have concluded they were a group of friends dining together. But if someone noticed him sitting with Wanda, they might get the wrong idea. And if they did, Cindy would hear of it before he got back to his condo. Fortunately, he didn't recognize anyone in the room.

"This is nice," Wanda said warmly. "I can't remember the last time we had dinner together." She reached to squeeze his hand, and a thrill shot up his arm. Why did she do that?

A server came, and they ordered glasses of wine. They discussed their sons and agreed they both appeared to be doing well. Wanda asked him about the investigation. Bill shared what he could but didn't mention Frank Richardi or killer drones. The wine came, they placed food orders, and the conversation turned to personal matters.

"So, let's discuss this woman you're seeing," said Wanda. "Her name is Cindy, right?"

Bill wrung his hands under the table. "Yes, Cindy. She's a nice person. I met her soon after I moved in. She lives in the next building."

"That's convenient." Wanda innocently sipped her wine.

Bill sensed she was toying with him. His ears grew warm. It seemed odd for him to share details of his new romantic interest with his ex-wife, but he'd never been good at keeping secrets from Wanda. Before long, he was recounting the awkwardness that had befallen Cindy and him when her son Justin decided to join the Coast Guard. But then the summer ended, and as temperatures dropped with the season's change, Cindy's relationship warmed up again.

"She sounds a bit flighty," said Wanda. "Like she can't make up her mind. Is that how you read her?"

Bill stared at his wine glass. "Yes, but I don't blame her for being unsure about making a commitment." Then he gazed at Wanda. "I feel the same way."

Wanda nodded. Perhaps she held similar feelings. Their marriage had its bad moments, but on the whole, Bill remembered those years with great fondness and wouldn't trade them for anything. If he could snap his fingers and be happily married again, he would. But getting from his current position to there seemed a long and arduous journey. It was easier to stay in the same place.

"Have you ever considered whether you and I should try again?" she said.

Bill pulled his shoulders back. Was she serious?

Wanda held up a hand. "It's a question, Bill. Not a proposal. Did the notion ever cross your mind?"

"You go first," he said.

Yes. Wanda had given the question considerable thought,

particularly at night when she remembered how it felt to be with someone she could count on. But they had both changed considerably from who they were when they met in their twenties. Also, five years had passed since the divorce, and they had been with others. Still, Wanda admitted that she had yet to meet anyone she admired or cared for as much as Bill.

Bill's hands tingled when Wanda confessed that she still cared for him.

"And yet, there is a big problem with us getting together," she said.

"What's that?"

"Location. You've moved on from South Carolina. My friends and work are there, but I can't see you ever moving back to Columbia. Can you?"

Bill bit his lip and pondered Wanda's question. Would he trade Wintergreen for another chance with Wanda? Move back to the city, with its concrete and traffic and noise? Then the motion of someone entering the restaurant caught his eye. He saw who it was and grew dizzy. Cindy and Phyllis Spooner chatted briefly with the hostess and then entered the dining room. Oh, jeez. There were only two open tables, and one was a few feet away. Bill tore his eyes from Cindy and clutched his napkin-wrapped cutlery.

"What's the matter?" said Wanda. "Oh, my, is that her? Cindy? The blonde?"

"Y-yes."

Wanda chuckled. "Goodness. They're headed our way."

Then Cindy noticed Bill, and she stopped to stare. The hostess made a beeline for the nearby table, but after a moment's hesitation, Cindy grabbed the hostess's attention and pointed at the table across the room.

"Whew," said Wanda. "That was a close call."

"We're not out of the clouds yet," he said.

After the hostess departed, Cindy said something to Phyllis, and the two women walked toward Bill's table.

Bill tried swallowing, but his mouth was dry. He reached for his water glass.

Then Cindy was at his side.

"Hi, Bill," she said with a tight smile. Her eyes cut to Wanda.

"Ah, yes," said Bill. "Hi, Cindy. Phyllis. This is m-my ex-wife, Wanda."

Cindy exaggerated her nod. "Oh, it's nice to meet you." Cindy paused to glare at Bill. "I'm Bill's . . . neighbor."

Wanda extended her hand with a genuine smile. "A pleasure. Bill's been telling me *all* about you."

Cindy nodded again. "I see."

Heat rushed up Bill's neck to his face. He might have a heart attack then and there.

But Phyllis saved the day by stepping forward. "I'm Bill's neighbor too." Phyllis also shook Wanda's hand, and the two women exchanged good-natured greetings. Then, Phyllis said to Bill, "I wanted to let you know that Nikki Churchill stayed with me the last two nights. She needed some company then but has now returned to her condo unit. The pain from her arm is much better, and she is ready to start moving forward. With Cassandra gone, she has to find a new job."

"Yes, I know," said Bill.

"She's a talented girl, and the job market is strong, so she'll have no trouble. I'll check on her again tomorrow."

Bill thanked Phyllis for her kindness, and the two women retreated to their table.

The rest of the meal was little more than a blur. Bill tried focusing on his food, but despite his efforts, he occasionally glanced toward Cindy's table. Engrossed in her conversation with Phyllis, Cindy appeared oblivious to Bill's presence.

He pulled on his shirt collar. "Does it seem warm in here to you?"

"Not particularly," said Wanda.

Wanda provided news of mutual friends of theirs in Columbia. Bill feigned interest and asked a few questions but was awfully glad when the plates were cleared and the check paid. Wanda and he rose, and he waited for her to collect her purse. When she straightened, instead of turning toward the door, she thanked Bill for inviting her to dinner, gave him a big smile, and then spontaneously kissed his lips in front of the entire restaurant.

Bill was stunned.

Before he could react, Wanda grabbed his hand and literally pulled him from the dining room. On the way out, he glanced nervously toward Cindy's table, hoping she had missed the PDA. No luck. Cindy's lips were a flat line, and her eyes seared into Bill.

Outside, still holding Bill's hand, Wanda laughed as they strolled onto the driveway.

"Why did you kiss me like that?" said Bill.

"It was premeditated. I was doing you a favor."

"A favor?"

Wanda paused and held both of Bill's hands. "You care for me, right?"

"Yes, you know I do."

"But you care for Cindy in a different kind of way. I can read it on your face when you look at her. She doesn't want to commit, and that's fair enough. It's a free and open dating world, even for later-stage singles like us. But sometimes it pays to let people know you have other options."

THIRTY-FIVE

Nevertheless, Bill worried about Cindy's reaction to Wanda and him kissing at the Devils Grill, so much so that when he took Curly out to stretch his legs, Bill scarcely noticed that low clouds had crept over Wintergreen. Much of the snow had melted, but patches remained behind shrubs and under eaves. Curly led Bill on a familiar route to the slope's edge behind the condo building. The lights from the Mountain Inn were diffused by mist. A man and woman conversed quietly on an upper balcony. Curly sniffed dead grass.

Inside, Bill tried watching television but could hardly follow the plot. He kept checking his phone for the time. By nine thirty, Bill was confident Cindy and Phyllis had finished dinner and returned to their homes. He stepped onto his balcony and glanced right to verify that the light was on in Cindy's living room. She was home.

Bill considered a phone call but decided the matter was best handled in person. At Cindy's door, he knocked twice and waited. Soft footsteps approached.

"Who's there?"

"It's me. Bill."

Cindy opened the door halfway and leaned against it. She had changed into old jeans and a long-sleeved T-shirt. Her sandy blond curls touched her shoulders, and the jeans hugged her hips. She seemed more tired than angry.

"What's up?" she said.

"I, uh, wanted to explain the kiss."

"Ah, yes. The kiss. The embers of South Carolinian romance continue to burn."

"That's not what it was about."

"Oh? Please, enlighten me."

Usually, Cindy would have invited him in by now. Not a good sign. Bill rubbed the back of his neck and then launched into an awkward recital of his dinner conversation with Wanda. Perhaps he had shared too much with Wanda concerning Cindy and Bill's romantic roller coaster ride.

Cindy stood straight and scowled. "Just what did you share?"

Bill held his hands up. "Nothing intimate, I assure you. Anyway, bottom line, Wanda kissed me to make you jealous."

Slowly, Cindy's eyes softened, and then her neck and shoulder muscles relaxed. "Well, it worked. I *am* jealous."

"You are?"

She stepped into the stairwell landing and put her arms around his neck. Bill touched her sides, and she nestled against him.

"I want my own kiss," she said.

Their kiss was warm and moist and lasted a lot longer than the one Wanda had given Bill at the Devils Grill.

Cindy pulled away and said, "Do you want to come in for a while?"

"I can't stay long," said Bill. "Curly needs to go out once more tonight."

Cindy placed her hand flat on Bill's chest.

Tingles spread throughout his body.

"It doesn't have to be for a long time. We'll make it a short visit."

Ninety minutes later, Bill exited Cindy's condo building humming a tune. At the sidewalk, he turned right. A short flight of wooden stairs cut through a small stand of trees that lay between their two condo buildings. Halfway down the stairs, a twig snapped on Bill's left, and he stopped. The staircase lights were too small to carry into the trees, and Bill squinted at the darkness. A footstep crunched frozen snow. Fine hairs stood on Bill's neck, and his heart rate accelerated.

"Hello? Who's there?"

No answer.

Bill retraced his steps to Cindy's parking lot. A figure moved on the other side of the trees.

"Hello?"

Bill stepped cautiously toward Blue Ridge Drive. A shadow crossed the lot farther down and entered the woods opposite Bill's building. Bill jogged forward. A crashing sound came from the woods.

"Wait! Stop!"

Bill slipped on an icy patch, fell, and banged his elbow. He rose slowly and then lumbered to the woods' edge. The crashing stopped. Whatever or whoever it was had cleared the woods and reached Blue Ridge Drive. Bill hurried to his Mazda and searched the neighborhood without success. Perspiration drenched the T-shirt he wore beneath his sweater. He returned home in the Mazda and sat in the SUV until his breathing settled. What was that? Not a bear, for they were all sleeping in their dens. Too big for a coyote. No, it was a person. And Bill could think of only one explanation.

The murderer was watching him.

THIRTY-SIX

Before seven o'clock the next morning, two developments occurred. First, Bill received a text from Chas Skibinski, the owner of the drone show company. Chas had new information but wanted to meet away from any place his employees might see him. Bill suggested they meet at Bill's condo at eight. Next, Skip Forrester informed Bill that he was now in Wintergreen. Knowing that Skip had come because of the drone angle, Bill invited him for breakfast and to hear from Skibinski firsthand.

When a confident knock sounded at Bill's front door, Curly commenced barking and scurried to the entrance.

"What do we have here?" said Skip Forrester. "A ferocious guard dog?"

"Meet Curly," said Bill.

Skip—who was a tall man with an athletic build—crouched to scratch behind Curly's ears. Curly wagged his tail so furiously his whole body shimmied.

"House rules," said Bill. "After greeting Curly, you must remove your shoes." Bill pointed to a small mat where a pair of his boots lay with open laces. "It's the only way to keep the floors clean in the winter. Want coffee?"

"Yes, please."

"Cereal? Oatmeal? Or eggs?" asked Bill.

"I'll have what you're having."

Bill fixed bowls of oatmeal in the microwave and laid out an assortment of goodies to dress their breakfast: raisins, chopped walnuts, brown sugar, and almond milk. While they ate at the kitchen counter, Bill brought Skip up to speed on Chas Skibinski's role as a drone entrepreneur and evangelist.

"Get this," said Bill. "They call him the Drone King."

Skip Forrester chuckled. "I hope he doesn't drone on all day."

Bill gave that some thought. "No. Actually, he's reasonably succinct."

"Good. I dislike sources who pontificate."

Skibinski arrived at eight, and the three men sat around the dining table. Curly listened from his bed next to the fireplace. Skibinski began by explaining how difficult it was for him to ask his employees about black market drone sales without raising suspicion.

"And Wintergreen appreciates your help," said Bill. "Now, if we could get to the contacts you've discovered."

"I bought a lot of drinks at the Edge last night to get this information," said Skibinski. "Now I feel exposed. I barely know one of these guys."

Bill almost responded with a snide response but stopped himself in time. Instead, Bill offered his genuine thanks and promised to reimburse Chas for the bar tab.

Chas pulled a folded piece of paper from his shirt pocket. "I have two names and two cell numbers. Both guys are staying in condos near the Mountain Inn."

"Excellent," said Bill. "Tell us about them."

Chas said the first name might be the guy they were searching for. Chas had hired him the previous week on a freelance basis. He had solid credentials and passed the background check, but Chas didn't like him because no one on Chas's team liked him. He was the kind of guy who could suck all of the enthusiasm from a room in a matter of minutes.

The second man came from the Midwest and was a genius at constructing drones to carry out particular tasks.

"Apparently, he's dabbled in drone hunting for wild pigs," said Chas.

Skip leaned forward. "To clarify, do you mean the drone spots the pigs for the hunter? Or the drone actually takes the shot?"

Chas heaved a sigh. "The drone carries a rifle that fires at the pig. The hunter operates the drone remotely and presses a button to tell the drone when it's okay to fire."

Skip asked Chas to describe the specific technology used, but Chas didn't know the answer. Chas said he only added the second man's name to be thorough. He personally knew the man, liked him, and didn't believe he would ever sell such a machine to another person.

"Mark is carbon-copy Midwest," said Chas. "He's a nice guy."

"Sure," said Skip. "He hunts wild pigs without giving them a chance. Nice."

THIRTY-SEVEN

E mily called another meeting for nine o'clock that morning, and when the parties assembled, Bill sensed a higher level of tension in the room. They were running out of time. The Nelson County Sheriff had asked Cassandra Key's retreat guests to remain in Wintergreen for follow-up questions, and they had all agreed. Still, people like Elsie Dale, Bryan McCasland, and Kent Olsen had limited patience.

Perhaps because he sensed the importance of time, Undersheriff Arnie Shields drove up to Wintergreen for the meeting. Emily Powell, Skip Forrester, and Bill sat at the conference table with Arnie, and Krista and Mitch stood on either side of the conference room door. Everyone was in uniform except for Bill and Skip Forrester.

Emily started the meeting by saying, "We have a new person joining the team." Then, she asked Skip to introduce himself and share what he knew about Frank Richardi.

As Skip gave his report, Bill observed the others in the room. Emily Powell seemed tired. With three young kids at home, it was a miracle she made it in to the office. Mitch stood relaxed against the wall. Krista's eyes were glued to

Skip, as if every word he spoke was critical to her under-standing of the case. Krista had aspirations for her career, and she was playing a more important role in this investigation than before.

Bill was only half listening to Skip because they had discussed the topic earlier, but then Skip mentioned the CIA.

"Wait," Bill said. "What was that?"

"It's not substantiated, but one guy who studied Richardi told me they suspect the CIA hired him once."

"That sounds like BS," said Bill.

Skip shrugged. "Could be. We know for a fact that he's worked for organized crime."

While Skip continued with his report, Bill considered the CIA angle. The State Department and the CIA often shared facilities in overseas locations. And they shared information and resources.

When Skip had finished, Emily thanked him for his report and said she had other news. "A forensics specialist spent much of the last two days going through Ms. Key's rental unit. The specialist found DNA and trace evidence of the person who was there the night before Key's death."

"We have a good idea of who that was," said Bill. He shared Kim Wiley's tip that Kent Olsen had dinner with Key the night before her death. "I'll press Olsen on the issue later this morning."

Arnie Shields nodded his approval.

Emily asked Bill, "So, what did you get from the Drone King?"

Bill shared what he'd learned from Chas Skibinski and then said, "The way I see it, we have the opportunity to progress on two paths: find the drone supplier and/or find the person who hired Richardi."

"Can you run down the suspect list and possible motives?" said Arnie.

"You bet," said Bill.

First up was Kent Olsen, vice president of the board. Kent had an affair with Cassandra several years ago and was now engaged to a timber and paper fortune heiress. But it appeared that Kent had continued to see Cassandra on the sly. Cassandra may have told Kent she would reveal their affair to the heiress, which would have threatened Kent's financial well-being.

"Okay," said Emily. "Who's next?"

Second up was Bryan McCasland, the board treasurer. From his first interview, Bill concluded that McCasland badly wanted the top slot. Now that Cassandra was dead, he could make his move.

"Nice guy," said Arnie.

"He's hard to like," said Bill.

The third suspect was Elsie Dale, the heiress. She had political aspirations and the money to hire a guy like Richardi.

"Why would she kill Key?" said Emily.

"I don't know," said Bill. "Cassandra had a run-in with Dale's company that drove hard feelings. And Elsie may have learned of Cassandra's ongoing affair with Kent Olsen. If so, maybe Elsie decided it was time for Cassandra to go."

Emily frowned, not impressed. Neither was Bill. These motives were all plausible, but murder seemed an awfully extreme measure. Then again, he'd been a homicide detective for twenty years and never encountered what he'd call a legitimate motive for murder.

"Any other suspects?" said Arnie.

"Nikki Churchill," said Bill.

The motives for the first three suspects were admittedly

weak, but he had trouble articulating any justification for Nikki to kill Cassandra. Still, he tried. Cassandra Key was a difficult boss. She argued with people for fun, and she belittled those she considered beneath her. Who knew what went on between superior and subordinate behind closed doors?

"But why would Nikki report Cassandra Key missing if she knew Key was dead?" said Mitch.

"To throw us a curve ball," said Bill.

"And the broken arm?" said Krista. "Did she take that fall intentionally?"

Bill shook his head. "No. I was there. That was a real accident."

"How do the alibis check out?" asked Emily.

Bill could have answered but nodded at Mitch for him to take the lead. Mitch stood straight and consulted his notes.

"The two men on the board of trustees—Olsen and McCasland—each stated they were working in their condo units. Neither of those alibis can be verified. Elsie Dale drove up from Chesapeake that morning and bought gas at a Shell station in Short Pump. The station has a record of the transaction, but the time stamp says eight-twenty-seven am, which is earlier than Dale remembered and early enough for her to reach Wintergreen before Ms. Key was killed. We haven't asked Nikki for an alibi yet. She was upset about the murder when we first spoke to her."

Arnie groaned and shook his head. "The alibi work doesn't help much. All of these guys had the opportunity, except for possibly the personal assistant."

"True," said Bill.

"And it could have been someone else altogether," said Arnie. "She was a difficult person, right?"

Bill held up a hand. "Yes, but someone must have helped Richardi identify Key that morning. That someone was here on the mountain and knew of Cassandra's plans. Now, Nikki knew Key was going hiking that morning, but Key may have also shared her plans with Olsen. And finally, McCasland or Dale could have watched Key's condo until she came out and then radioed instructions to Richardi."

"I don't know," said Arnie. "We have an awful lot of conjecture going on here. It feels like this case is out of our grasp. What if Richardi wasn't after Cassandra Key at all? What if he made a mistake?"

Then we're done, Bill thought, but he kept his mouth shut. The possibility that the murderer's motive was simply to test the accuracy of a drone sniper had crossed Bill's mind. If so, the murderer might have killed Cassandra Key randomly. But who was the audience? Potential clients? And why involve Frank Richardi? No, that didn't work. The method read like a Frank Richardi special. Richardi, and whoever hired him, planned to kill Cassandra Key on this trip. The drone allowed Frank to carry out the hit remotely, and the drone's capabilities enabled it to compensate for bad weather. The team was on the right track, and it would pay off if they kept doing the grunt work.

"Arnie, don't be such a pessimist," said Emily with some irritation.

Arnie's eyes snapped to Emily, and it appeared he would offer a retort, but then his expression softened, and he nodded. "You're right. I get that way sometimes."

"Hey," said Skip. "I received an email a minute ago. I fed the two names we got from Skibinski to my task force. We have nothing on the dude from the Midwest, but the freelance guy is a winner. Gavin Gaines is his name, and he has contacts in military supply that we're already watching."

Emily nodded with enthusiasm. "Let's discuss assignments."

Skip Forrester was most interested in finding the person who had supplied the drone, so he was designated to follow up on the Skibinski leads. Krista Jackson would accompany Skip as a guide and driver. Bill and Mitch would circle back to the suspects they had interviewed earlier with follow-up questions. Emily would run coordination from the office and bring in resources as needed.

"Okay, boys and girls," said Emily. "Let's get it done."

THIRTY-EIGHT

Krista led Skip Forrester from the police station to where she had parked her orange Subaru. Her stomach was a jumbled mess, and her hands trembled slightly as she started the car and adjusted the heat controls. This was the first time she had escorted anyone from another law enforcement agency around the mountain. The FBI, no less.

For goodness' sake, don't screw it up.

Skip was tall and lanky with strong hands. When he sat in the front seat, his knees jutted into the air.

"Oh, gosh, you're a lot taller than my son. The adjustment is beneath the seat front."

Skip slid the seat all the way back and then chuckled. He seemed a little on edge.

Krista pulled out of the parking lot and turned onto Wintergreen Drive.

"What should I call you?" she said. "Agent Forrester?"

Skip arched his eyebrows. "Please don't. I'll be forced to leave the car and hike the mountain alone."

Krista laughed, relieved. He had a sense of humor.

"Skip, then," she said.

"Thank you. And you? Should I call you Krista?"

She frowned. "No, actually, I prefer Officer Jackson."

With his eyebrows stitched together, Skip's dark eyes read her expression. Krista turned her face forward and tried to keep her lips pressed together, but then she burst out laughing.

Skip smiled. "So that's how it is, huh?"

"Yep. We like to keep things formal here in Wintergreen."

They rode in silence for the next mile. The road was mostly cleared of snow, but a few icy patches remained in spots shaded by the mountain. Krista kept her hands at ten and two.

"Do you like your Subaru?" asked Skip, perhaps to make conversation.

"I love it. It's four years old but runs like brand new."

"It's climbing this mountain with no trouble."

Krista nodded. "I got the turbo engine on my ex-husband's recommendation, and I'm glad I did. Tyler has his issues—no question—but he sure knows cars. And that brings me to an observation that I simply must make."

Skip cocked an eyebrow. "Okay. Let me hear it."

"This is the first time I've had a Forrester in my Forester."

Skip groaned. Krista laughed again, and he soon joined her.

"Are you going to do this all day?" he said. "The corny jokes?"

"No. Well, maybe. But only if they're super corny."

Okay, thought Krista, *that's enough silly humor and enough sharing of personal information.*

Skip now knew she had at least one kid and was divorced. Krista wondered whether Skip was married. No ring, but that didn't mean much. Tyler had never worn a wedding ring.

The FBI agent wasn't bad-looking. She guessed he was in his mid-to-late thirties, about her age. His hair was turning prematurely gray, and he wore a three-day scruff beard that made him appear rugged. His dark eyes absorbed everything around him with ease. In the meeting with Emily and the others, Skip had come across as a professional who knew his craft. Articulate and insightful, he had earned Bill O'Shea's respect when they worked on other cases, which was good enough for Krista.

Midway up the mountain, Wintergreen Drive made several sharp turns, and the incline angle increased. Her Forester responded to the challenge with ease.

"What do you think of Bill's theory that Cassandra Key was killed by a drone?" Skip asked.

"Why? Do you have reason to doubt him?"

"Not particularly. But I wanted to hear your opinion as well."

"Oh." As she was only a communications officer, the higher-ups didn't always solicit her views, which made sense to Krista. That's why they were the higher-ups. But of course, she did have opinions and was ready to share them when asked. "I would consider Bill's killer drone hypothesis far-fetched except for two factors. First, the storm was so fierce that even a skilled sniper couldn't make the shot, but for a sophisticated targeting machine? No problem."

"Okay. And the second factor?"

"The truck and trailer sighting Mitch discovered in Charlottesville. The witness's description closely matches the truck and trailer Art Rossi saw at the top of Old Stoney Creek Road two hours later. Those two sightings must be connected."

"I agree," said Skip.

"But it still reads like science fiction. Are sniper drones actually available on the black market?"

"No. But similar weapons might soon be. That's why I'm here."

Skip described a trend feared by all federal security organizations—the growing threat of low-cost, high-tech weapons that modestly funded bad actors could afford. For example, remotely operated drones using facial recognition technology could potentially assassinate politicians. Skip cited other high-tech instruments of destruction.

"Engineered viruses. Utility disruptions via cyberattack. Fully autonomous weapons. It's a nightmare."

"What's our plan for this guy? Gavin Gaines."

"Start with easy questions and sniff his answers. If they smell bad, we ask harder questions."

"What if he won't say anything?"

Krista glanced at Skip and caught him looking at her. His gaze lingered, and she got the impression he was assessing her appearance. Her cheeks grew warm, and she turned her eyes back to the road. What was that all about? And why was she embarrassed?

Skip answered, "No matter what Gaines says, we'll know more than we know now."

THIRTY-NINE

B ill texted Nikki Churchill on the way up the mountain to see if it was convenient for her to meet. It was. Mitch pulled the squad car into the reception lot of the Mountain Inn right behind Krista's Subaru Forester. Once out of the car, Bill and Mitch waved at the other two, and the teams went their separate ways.

Inside the Mountain Inn, Bill and Mitch climbed the stairs to the upper floor and came upon Nikki conferring with another woman in the hallway. The men stopped short to give the two women some privacy. The second woman was about Nikki's height and wore the uniform of a resort employee. There appeared to be a language barrier that Nikki only overcame by miming the act of pulling something over her broken arm. The second woman eventually nodded her understanding and walked in Bill and Mitch's direction. According to the tag she wore on her shirt, her name was Maria, and she was from Guatemala.

"Everything okay?" Bill asked Nikki.

"Yes. You got here faster than I expected." Nikki gestured at her torso and legs with her free hand. "I've been sponge bathing for days and need to take a shower. I was headed downstairs to ask the front desk for a plastic bag when I ran into Maria. She's going to find one for me."

"Can we talk now?" said Bill.

"Oh, yeah. I don't smell or anything." Nikki laughed. "At least, I don't believe so. But let's go outside just in case."

Bill smiled, and a light feeling entered his chest. Nikki was in much better spirits than when Bill and Mitch told her of Cassandra's death.

Outside, the cold air assaulted them. Nikki wore a dark blue puffer coat with one side draped over her shoulder. After Bill helped her pull the zipper up, they walked onto the brick patio and watched skiers trudge toward the slope in their boots. Once on the snow with their skis fastened, the skiers poled forward until gravity took over and pulled them into their first run of the day.

"By the way," said Nikki. "Thank you for sending Mrs. Spooner my way. After breaking my arm and learning of Cassandra's murder, I was a mess. I actually spent two nights at Phyllis's place. She was a godsend."

"Have you figured out what you're going to do next?" asked Bill.

Nikki's face brightened. "Yes, I have. I've been in touch with Cassandra's sister, who inherited her gun shop chain. Her sister wants to keep the business and has asked me to stay on."

"That's excellent," said Bill.

But Nikki's smile quickly disappeared. "When I remember that she's gone, it doesn't feel right for me to be happy again."

Bill nodded that he understood. "Even so, you have to keep living. One foot in front of the other."

Mitch cleared his throat, reminding Bill that they had a lot of ground to cover.

Bill told Nikki they were still working on the investigation and needed to circle back with her on a few items. Naturally, as part of the process, they needed to know where everyone was at the time of the murder.

"Can you tell us where you were that morning?" said Bill.

Nikki's eyebrows knitted together. "Oh, I know. I had planned to drive down to see Staunton because I heard it's a cute town. But the weather forecast was so bad I stayed up here. I tried going for a walk, but the wind and snow forced me back inside, and I worked until I got hungry. I ate lunch at the Edge and then drove to Blackrock Circle, where I was supposed to meet Cassandra."

"Did you speak with anyone at the Edge?" asked Mitch.

Nikki pushed her lips out. "I spoke with my server, but I don't know if she would remember me."

Mitch nodded and said that was no problem.

Bill realized that he and Mitch were treating Nikki with kid gloves. Why? Probably her youth and position. Also, the broken arm. Plus, the fact that he couldn't fathom a legitimate motive for her. But he warned himself to be wary of blind spots. He'd come across plenty of youthful murderers in his career, and Nikki had not broken her arm until after Cassandra's death. But the lack of motive was still an issue.

"Have you thought of anything else that could help us with the investigation?" he asked.

Nikki's eyes darted to the nearby skiers. She chewed on her lip. "Maybe. Do you remember you told me someone was in Cassandra's condo the night before her death? And I told you I didn't know who that might be?"

"Yes."

"I wasn't being completely truthful."

"Okay," said Bill. "Let's hear it."

Nikki rubbed the back of her neck.

She was near the same age as Bill's son Matt, perhaps a few years older. Bill hoped Matt didn't have to go through something like this anytime soon.

"I don't know for sure who was with Cassandra, but I suspect it was Kent Olsen. I didn't want to put Cassandra in a bad light after her death, but I knew that the two of them were still carrying on. It was supposed to be a secret, but as her personal assistant, I knew pretty much everything she did."

"Who else knew?" said Bill.

"Elsie Dale might have known. Cassandra dated more than a few men in the years I worked for her—some men longer than others. She never cared who learned of her affairs. If Elsie suspected anything, it wouldn't have been hard for her to discover the truth."

Bill nodded and glanced at Mitch.

Mitch raised his eyebrows.

Nikki had no other information and asked Bill if she could now leave Wintergreen. She wished to return to Norfolk to begin her new position working for Cassandra's sister.

"I understand," said Bill. "Could you stay one more day in case something else comes up?"

"Yes, of course. I can get a lot of work done online."

"It must be slow typing with one hand," said Mitch.

Nikki pulled her broken arm into an awkward position, bringing her two hands together in front of her belly. "My fingers work fine, so I can type. And fortunately, I'm left-handed. That certainly helps."

At that moment, Bill thought of another question. Two pieces of data he'd acquired during the investigation struck him as oddly coincidental. Chas Skibinski said the drone show was postponed a week, which caused Chas to spend extra money on preparations. And earlier, Bryan McCasland had complained that the retreat was pushed back a week. Bill asked Nikki what caused the delay.

Nikki shrugged in a what-can-you-do expression. "That was Cassandra. It was a pain in the behind to move everything around, but Cassandra was forever changing her schedule at the last minute."

Bill thanked Nikki for her time. The schedule change was a curious coincidence that didn't seem to fit with the rest of the data. Maybe it meant nothing at all.

∾

Standing beside the squad car, Mitch folded his arms and said to Bill, "So, the plot thickens, right?"

"Yeah."

"Kent Olsen is engaged to one of the richest women in Virginia, but he's still fooling around with Cassandra Key. Ms. Dale finds out about it and then what? She contacts Frank Richardi?"

"It's possible. Ms. Dale could afford it. Maybe she found Richardi online."

"Where? Assassinsforhire.com?"

"Maybe a dark web chatroom."

Mitch frowned. "Seems a bit sci-fi for Wintergreen."

Bill checked his phone for the time. They had a follow-up interview with Kent Olsen in a few minutes. "Let's see what Mr. Olsen has to say."

FORTY

K rista and Skip first tried to find Gavin Gaines. As an army veteran with contacts in military supply units, Gaines might have access to stolen weapons. Skip tried calling Gaines's phone with no luck. According to Chas Skibinski's intel, Gaines was staying in one of Timbers condos near the Mountain Inn.

Krista pulled her Subaru into the Mountain Inn's reception lot ahead of Mitch and Bill, who were there to interview Nikki Churchill again. Krista and Skip waved at the other two, and then Krista led Skip toward the Timbers.

Gavin Gaines's room was on the second floor. At the door, Krista knocked, and they waited. And waited. Krista's second knock met with the same result.

"Maybe he saw you coming and stepped out the other way," said Krista. "You do look intimidating."

"Me? You're the one in uniform."

"What should we do now?"

They had phoned Skibinski's second contact and had an appointment to meet him at the Terrace Café in forty minutes. To kill time, they went to the Mountain Inn and got coffees, and then Skip excused himself to call his home office.

Rather than standing in the lounge attracting attention with her uniform, Krista strolled out front and down the sidewalk. A young woman and two little girls in ski apparel struggled to climb from a lower parking lot while carrying skis and poles. When the little girls noticed Krista, they stopped to stare.

"How y'all doing?" said Krista.

The woman smiled and said, "Fine. We're slowly making our way to the slopes."

"Are you a policeman?" said the smaller of the two girls.

"A police *officer*," said the woman.

"Yes," said Krista.

"I want to be a police officer when I grow up," said the same girl.

The other girl, who Krista guessed was the shyer of the two, simply smiled.

"Can I give you folks a hand with your gear?"

"No, we're good," said the woman. "I know you're busy."

Krista reached to grab skis from one girl and then the other. "It's no problem. I'm on a break."

As they made their way around the lodge to the ticket counter, Krista continued her conversation with the group. The girls were curious. Did Krista drive a police car? Not often. She mainly worked in the office. Did she like her job? Yes, very much. Did she live in Wintergreen? No, she lived in Nellysford.

"I'm sorry they're asking so many questions," said the woman.

"Don't worry. I have two boys myself. It's nice to chat with girls once in a while."

At the top of the slope, the little girls and the woman

donned their skis, waved, and then set off down the most accessible trail.

Turning around, Krista noticed Mitch, Bill, and Nikki Churchill walking back into the lodge. With another half hour to kill, she spent the time watching skiers begin their day.

The lounge had tables and chairs enough for several dozen people to relax, but by that time of the day, most of the guests had moved on to other activities. Propane-fueled flames licked at lava rocks in the fireplace. A man in a comfortable armchair typed on his laptop. Two women conversed quietly at a table on the other side of the room. Krista and Skip chose to sit at a small table off to one side.

A prematurely balding man who appeared to be in his mid-thirties approached their table and introduced himself as Mark Woodland. Krista's first impression of Woodland was favorable because he had a ready smile and a firm handshake.

Woodward was more than willing to answer any and all questions they posed. Yes, he was aware of the murder on the mountain. Yes, he had heard rumors that a drone fired the shot that killed the victim. Yes, he built drones by hand to hunt wild pigs.

"But it's not by choice," he said. "The work I do for farmers is the lesser of two evils."

"How's that?" said Skip.

"Feral hogs destroy crops worth billions annually. A female pig can have two litters per year with ten piglets in each litter. What can a farming family do? They can't take time off to hunt pigs, and even if they did, they couldn't keep up."

"You built a drone that shoots pigs from the air?" said Skip.

"Yes, I did."

"Do you realize that's against the law?"

"Yes, but no one's prosecuted me yet, and I don't think they will."

Skip asked Mark how he had constructed his pig-killing drone. Mark was articulate and succinct with his responses. He had a gift of making complex technology appear straight-forward. The drones' sensors used thermal imaging tech-nology to detect a wild pig's position, the direction of motion, and speed. Prevailing wind and other factors were taken into consideration. The software understood the exact capabilities of the mounted hunting rifle and could quickly make fine-tuned adjustments to the drone's aiming position. The drone could fire the gun, adjust its aim, and repeat the process several times each second. Pigs had little to no chance of surviving an encounter with Mark's drone.

"I gather your drone could as easily fire upon and kill a human," said Skip.

A pained expression came over Mark's face. "That could never happen."

"How can you say that? Where is your drone now?"

"Locked in my garage in the Wichita suburbs. The computer that drives the drone's operation is locked in a wall safe. On top of that, getting through the program's security requires a password, my fingerprint, and my face."

Skip nodded and then asked Krista if she had additional questions. She didn't.

They thanked Mark for his time, and he left.

Of course, Mark might have been lying. Frank Richardi may have contacted him on the sly and paid him handsomely to bring his drone to Wintergreen. But Krista would have bet a month's salary against that scenario. Skip said he felt the same way.

Then Skip said, "What do you say? Should we try Mr. Gaines again?"

"Definitely."

FORTY-ONE

B ill stood in the hallway outside of Kent Olsen's rented condo and assessed the view. The Highlands Express chairlift ended a hundred yards from where he stood. Skiers dismounted, shot down the off-ramp, and then paused at the top of the hill to pick the slope they would ski next—Outer Limits to the left, Wild Turkey down the middle, or Cliffhanger to the right. Light-gray clouds hung heavy in the sky. Snowflakes fluttered softly to the ground.

Kent Olsen had a perfect view of where Loggers Alley Trail crossed the Wild Turkey ski run. Had he known Cassandra Key would hike across the mountain that morning? Had he directed Frank Richardi from his condo unit? They could have used two-way radios for communication.

In his mind, Bill recreated the scene on Cassandra Key's final morning. The clouds were lower and the wind higher. Resort operations had closed the mountain, so the lift was silent. Six-person chairs rocked in the wind. Clouds blew across the face of the mountain, causing the chairlift support towers and cables to come in and out of view. Then, the clouds parted, and four hundred yards in the distance, a woman wearing an orange jacket hiked from the woods onto the ski slope. A drone dipped out of a cloud and took aim.

Bang. Bang.

"You want me to knock?" said Mitch.

Bill startled and then blinked several times. "Yes."

Elsie Dale was down in Crozet meeting with a realtor, which suited Bill fine. He'd rather interview Kent Olsen alone.

"Are you two considering moving here?" asked Bill.

"It's a second residence opportunity," said Kent. "Actually, it would be Elsie's fourth home. She wants to buy a horse farm in Albemarle Country. She attended UVA and likes coming back for football games, reunions, and such."

"Gotcha," said Bill. Guess a regular upscale hotel wouldn't do. He felt sorry for rich folks who couldn't resist spending money on possessions that would consume more of their time. Better to live in a simple condo with a beautiful view.

"When's the wedding?" said Mitch.

The three of them sat in the living area around a coffee table. Kent had offered cups of coffee, and they both accepted.

Kent shook his head. "Only two months away. I can't believe it. The engagement has flown by."

Bill nodded and then said, "Ms. Dale is living a charmed life. She's wealthy, attractive, and has an exciting political future."

"She has an excellent chance of winning this next election," said Kent.

Bill spread his hands in a grand gesture. "Who knows how far she could go? Maybe even the White House."

Kent's eyebrows shot up. "Whoa. Let's not get ahead of

ourselves." He chuckled nervously, as if the thought had crossed his mind, but he didn't want to jinx it.

"What I can't understand," said Bill, "is why you would risk all that by sleeping with Cassandra Key."

An indignant frown crossed Kent's face, and he glared at Bill. "That's an absurd accusation. Why would you say that?"

"Here you are, a junior diplomat with the State Department, and you've landed the dream bride. Money. Power. Influence. And you're willing to throw all that away to fool around with an old girlfriend. I don't get that."

"But that's not true. Stop saying that."

"Come now," said Bill. "Let's not play games. Cassandra Key is dead. And we have DNA proof that you were in her bed the night before she was killed." Bill stretched the truth a bit, but he was confident the forensic tests would back up his statement.

"But . . ." Kent's eyes darted to Mitch.

Mitch nodded to confirm Bill's statement.

Kent lifted a hand to his face. His fingers trembled.

"I'm waiting," said Bill. "Why would you do that? One last fling with an old lover? Was that it?"

Kent stammered, "I . . . I . . ."

But then it all made sense to Bill. Kent's motive for killing Cassandra Key. He was an addict removing the source of his addiction.

"Now I get it," said Bill. "You couldn't resist her, and Cassandra taunted you with that knowledge. She played with your emotions. You knew that sooner or later Elsie would find out, and you couldn't risk that."

Kent shook his head violently.

"You knew you couldn't make the shot yourself," said Bill. "It was far too risky, and you're not that good of a shot anyway. So you stood on your balcony and watched for Cassandra."

Kent's eyes bugged open.

Bill was on a roll. "You knew she would hike across Loggers Alley Trail that day, because you had discussed it the night before. You spied her orange jacket through the swirling snow and signaled the killer to take the shot."

"What are you talking about? What killer?" said Kent. "I didn't do any of that stuff. Well, I did watch for her—you have that right—but I never saw her because of the storm. She had told me she was doing a rigorous hike, and I knew her route. Cassandra asked me to join her, but I had to work."

"Sorry, Mr. Olsen," said Mitch. "I don't believe you."

"You've had dealings with the CIA before," said Bill. "Haven't you?"

Kent's eyes flitted between Bill and Mitch; he was panicking now. "I don't understand. Yes, I've worked with the CIA on occasion. We're co-located in offices around the world. Why is that relevant?"

"And you've come across Frank Richardi," said Bill. "Maybe worked with him once."

Kent's face grew tight, and he narrowed his eyes. "Who's Frank Richardi?"

"The killer you hired. Richardi used a drone to do the job. Maybe you were involved in that part. Maybe not." Bill pointed toward the balcony. "Either way, you stood there and gave Richardi a sign when Cassandra broke free of the woods."

The vice president clenched his teeth and leaned forward. "This is all new to me. Frank Richardi? A drone? I'm completely lost."

Bill had to admit Kent Olsen was a good actor, but Bill was in no mood to go easy on him.

Olsen cleared his throat and then cleared it again. "Okay. Let's slow it down a little. I admit that I lied about Cassandra. I went out with her the night before she died. It was to be our last evening together. I had no intention of sleeping with her, but . . ." Kent bobbed his head from side to side as if in doubt. "I am infuriated with myself for not being able to resist her, but I couldn't. You were right. I was addicted to her. I don't know why I was so drawn to her. I'll never know, but I would have done anything she asked. I wanted her to marry me. Even that night, if Cassandra had told me she wanted to be with me forever, I would have called off my marriage to Elsie." Kent Olsen's head hung low. "But Cassandra was playing with me, as always. She said she would never commit to me and I should marry Elsie. She told me to take the money—that I would live happily ever after. And she promised that if I ever got bored, she'd be there to spice things up."

"It's a moving story," said Bill, "but I'm not in the mood for a romance. You were in touch with Richardi. He said Wintergreen was a good location, and you suggested it to Cassandra."

"Wintergreen wasn't my idea," said Kent.

"Uh-huh," said Mitch. "Sure. And you just happened to get a rental condo with a fantastic view of Cassandra's route."

"Yes," said Kent. "That's true. It *was* random. I had no idea I would get this condo."

Mitch lifted an eyebrow in a supreme gesture of skepticism.

"You're looking at the wrong guy," said Kent. "You should question McCasland. He's obsessed with taking over the club's presidency. He's already campaigning. I got a blast email outlining his platform for growth. Members have complained to me. It's unbelievable. Maybe he did it."

Bill intended to interview McCasland next, but he would not share that with Olsen. Instead, he pointed his finger at the club vice president. "If you killed Cassandra, you should admit it now. Things will go easier for you. We'll catch you one way or another. We'll find the connection to Richardi or other evidence that ties you to the crime."

But Olsen wasn't paying attention. His eyes were filled with hope. "Ask McCasland what he did in the Air Force."

"Save us the trouble," said Bill.

"He flew combat drones."

Outside, Bill and Mitch exchanged notes. Despite Olsen's admission of spending the night with Key and the proximity of his rental condo to the murder scene, Bill and Mitch sensed the case still held more secrets.

FORTY-TWO

B ill and Mitch entered the Mountain Inn and headed toward the Terrace Café. A young family of four passed them in the lobby, and the children stared at Mitch in his uniform.

"How y'all doing?" said Mitch.

The children smiled, and the woman said, "Fine. Fine. How about you?"

"Awesome," said Mitch. "I'm inside, and it feels great."

They found Bryan McCasland sitting at a table off to one side of the coffee shop. He nursed a small coffee.

After brief greetings, McCasland said, "I hope this won't take long. I have nothing to add to our earlier discussion."

Jeez. Who would ever vote for this guy?

"Are you in a hurry to get somewhere?" said Bill.

McCasland rolled his eyes. "Yeah, like, get on with my life. The sheriff asked me to stick around, and I'm trying to be a good citizen, but enough is enough. I have a job to get back to."

"I thought you could work remotely," said Bill. "You said

on the day Ms. Key was killed, you were in your condo working hard on a proposal."

Bryan edged back in his chair. He had come out with guns blazing but was now reconsidering his approach. In a more accommodating voice, he said, "That's true. I was working."

"What's changed?" said Bill. "This is a murder investigation. If it's not about work, why are you in a hurry? What's so important for you to get back to, or are you trying to get *away* from something?"

"No, I didn't mean that. I want to be helpful, but at the same time, I want to get back to my routine. Surely, you can understand that."

Mitch nodded sagely.

"Yes," said Bill. "I can understand. There's an election coming up to fill the open position created by Ms. Key's death. If you're going to win—and you want to win badly— you have to crank up your campaign. Running a campaign is hard work. And you'll want to shake hands with influential members to cement their support."

Bryan scrunched his eyebrows. "Wait, surely you don't consider me a suspect."

"But we do," said Bill. "We consider you one of our prime suspects."

"Why would I kill her? What's my motive?"

"I'm not the smartest player on the team," said Mitch, "but even I know it's hard to lobby for the head coach position when the head coach is still there."

McCasland scowled. "That's absurd. It's just a silly club. No way I would kill Cassandra to take her place."

"Oh, I beg to differ," said Bill. "This is not just any club. The Old Virginia Gun Club carries a lot of prestige in the state. And you'd be *president*. It doesn't matter whether you are president of the United States or president of a bowling league. You still get to call the shots."

"I don't care about it that much."

"I think you do," said Bill. He leaned a bit closer to Bryan. "You'd be in charge. At work, you have to follow other people's orders. But as president, you'd give the orders."

McCasland folded his arms and pouted like a child.

"Didn't you tell me you could do a better job than Cassandra?" said Bill.

The treasurer chewed the inside of his lip. His eyes rolled suspiciously from Bill to Mitch.

Bill said, "You have ideas for how to plug the holes in the sinking ship, don't you?"

"Of course I do," said Bryan. "A moron could do a better job than Cassandra. The Old Virginia Gun Club was founded in 1952. My grandfather was in the club."

"It's personal," said Bill.

"Yes. The OVGC deserves better than Cassandra Key. She should have never been given the job because she alienated everyone and listened to no one. I can turn it around. Bring in new blood. Start growing again. The club could be strong for another hundred years."

"You're the right person for the job," said Bill.

"Yes."

"It's your time."

"Yes."

McCasland spat the word. He was caught up in it now.

"And Cassandra was standing in your way."

"Yes!"

Bill sat back to savor the moment. Obviously, McCasland desperately wanted Key out of the way. It was nearly a confession, and Bill waited for Bryan to fill in the blanks.

"You tricked me," said Bryan.

"I got you to say what you wanted to say," said Bill. "It wasn't hard, Bryan. You're wearing it like an angry red coat."

"I didn't kill her. I'd have difficulty making a four-hundred-yard shot in ideal conditions, let alone in the middle of a snowstorm."

"How did you know it was a four-hundred-yard shot?" said Bill. "I never told you that."

Bryan's mouth dropped. He blinked several times. "I don't know. Someone told me. Maybe it was Kent. Yeah, it was Kent."

Now that Bill had Bryan on edge, it was time to switch gears. Bryan acknowledged his motive, but they needed more to prove he committed the crime.

"You misled me earlier," said Bill, "when you told me you worked in logistics for the Air Force."

"No. I do work in logistics."

"But that's not what you did in active service. Not at all. You were a drone pilot who served in combat situations. Isn't that right?"

"So?"

"So, Cassandra Key was killed by a sniper drone."

McCasland frowned but then leaned back and rubbed his chin. A change came over his face. He seemed more relaxed. Bill sensed that McCasland wasn't concerned any longer. Why?

"A drone," McCasland said. "Yes, that makes a lot of sense. I couldn't see how a sniper would ever make that shot in the storm, but with a drone, the killer only had to lock onto the target and let the tech take over."

Bill said, "You can see how everything adds up to you being in the number one suspect position."

Bryan gave that consideration and then chuckled. "Yes.

You probably suspect I used my logistics connections to procure a sniper drone."

The notion had crossed Bill's mind, but Bryan was on a roll. Sometimes it paid to let the silence linger. Some suspects couldn't resist filling the quiet with new revelations.

"That kind of technology is not yet available on the Air Force buy list," said Bryan. "At least, it's not available to my team. But I know it exists. An Israeli company made an announcement not long ago. The robot weapon can be mounted on a drone and triggered by a remote operator. The technology uses a unique stabilization algorithm to accurately hit targets while moving. If one company has done it, others won't be far behind. This stuff is getting better all the time." Bryan's eyes lit up like a gamer contemplating a new release. "Truthfully, I could find such a drone on the black market. It wouldn't be hard. But I couldn't afford to buy it. A drone like that would cost millions."

"Maybe you could rent it," said Bill.

Bryan gazed up to the right and then rubbed his chin again. "Yes, I believe I could. That might only cost forty to fifty thousand." Then Bryan thrust his hand forward. "But not if the seller knew it would be used for murder. They wouldn't touch that. Ever. These guys have businesses to run."

"But you wouldn't necessarily tell them," said Mitch.

"No, of course not."

"Is that what you did?" said Bill. "Rent the drone that killed Cassandra Key?"

McCasland pressed his lips tightly together and eyed Bill and Mitch with disdain. "I've told you guys umpteen times that I didn't kill Cassandra, and I stand by that statement. If you still believe I'm guilty, try to prove it. You'll have a tough time."

Bryan held Bill's gaze without the slightest hesitation.

Though Bill continued to find the man distasteful, he was inclined to believe him. Even so, Bill would keep Bryan's name on the leaderboard until the final score was in. He'd known people who had lied their way out of many tight spots.

"On the other hand," said McCasland, "the last time we met, I gave you a good lead. Have you made any progress with that?"

"Elsie Dale?" said Bill.

"As I said before, a person with her kind of power, money, and trajectory might want to tie off a loose end. And something I heard last night underscored that initial thought."

"Okay," said Bill. "We're all ears."

"Last night, Elsie, Kent, and I had dinner together. I'm afraid my feelings about Cassandra's inept handling of the club became clear after two glasses of wine. Among other criticisms, I said I didn't believe Cassandra was trustworthy. Kent grew angry, but rather than laying into me, he excused himself to go to the restroom. After he left the room, Elsie turned to me and said, 'Cassandra was not the only one. You can't trust anyone anymore.'"

"That's interesting," said Bill.

"Maybe I'm wrong," said Bryan, "but I could swear Elsie meant that Kent and Cassandra had been carrying on an affair. Which would make sense in my view. Kent never got over Cassandra, and it would be just like Cassandra to take advantage of that."

"What do you think?" said Bill when he and Mitch were in the squad car heading down the mountain.

Mitch kept his eyes straight ahead and drove through two full turns of the curvy road before answering. "My gut tells me McCasland might be the bad guy, but I can't get there logically. In fact, there's a big problem with that answer."

"Go ahead. Spell it out."

Bill guessed that he and Mitch had hit the same obstacle when trying to pin the murder-one prize on McCasland, but he wanted Mitch to make his argument. People only got better at that kind of stuff with practice.

"McCasland and Richardi don't fit in the same picture," said Mitch. "McCasland knows how to fly drones himself. If he wanted to kill Cassandra Key with a drone, why would he need Richardi?"

"Exactly."

"I don't like McCasland as a person, but I doubt he's our guy."

"Maybe not," said Bill. "Let's hear what the heiress has to say."

FORTY-THREE

K rista and Skip tried Gaines's condo a second time without success, and he still wasn't answering his phone. Skip said finding Gaines was important enough that he wanted to wait and try again, so they sat in the Mountain Inn's lounge and talked. Krista asked Skip how he'd come to join the FBI. He'd studied accounting on an ROTC scholarship and then gotten involved with military intelligence while serving in the Navy. After four years of that, joining the FBI seemed a natural career progression. He applied and was accepted, and momentum took over.

Krista listened to Skip's story with great interest. Occasionally, she considered decisions she'd made early on that would affect the rest of her life. But her life wasn't over yet. Krista was taking online criminal justice courses to advance her career, and so far, her grades were excellent. She might never work for the FBI, but she still had many opportunities ahead.

After thirty minutes, they returned to the Timbers. Once inside the building, they took the stairwell on the left. Skip climbed two stairs at a time, and Krista hustled to keep up. At the top of the stairs, Skip turned right and nearly collided with a man wearing jeans, a heavy jacket, and a ball cap pulled low.

"Sorry, man," said Skip.

"No problem."

Skip turned right into the hallway and strode toward Gaines's room. The man in the jacket eyed Krista shyly from under his cap. He had a bushy mustache. She nodded at him.

"What's up?" he said.

"Nothing much. A routine check." Which she realized might have sounded strange to the man. The Wintergreen police never conducted routine checks of personal residences. They only came when called, but her answer must have been good enough because the man proceeded down the stairs without delay.

Skip knocked on the door, and they waited in silence. No footsteps sounded from inside.

Krista was going to say they could wait another hour and check again, but something tugged at her concentration. Most people who encountered a uniformed police officer would stop and stare for at least a moment before going about their business.

"Oh," she said. "Darn."

Adrenaline coursed through Krista's veins. She turned and ran toward the window at the end of the hall. On the ground, the man in the ballcap scampered across Wintergreen Drive to the lower parking lot. He glanced nervously back at the Timbers.

"That's him," she shouted. "Gaines."

The stairwell became a blur as she and Skip sprinted to the ground floor. Once outside, they ran toward the Mountain Inn reception lot. A dark Chrysler 300—which had to be Gaines's car—sped across the lower lot. At the exit, the

Chrysler spun gravel and entered Wintergreen Drive without stopping. Krista and Skip jumped into her Forester, and she gunned the engine. Her heart pounded. Before entering Wintergreen Drive, she pumped the brakes once to check for oncoming traffic and then accelerated down the hill.

"Call the station," she yelled.

"What's the number?"

Krista recited the number and gave Skip instructions on what to say to the officer who answered. There was only one route out of Wintergreen. If the police pulled two squad cars across the road, Gaines would have no place to go. Between Gaines and the entrance were over two miles of a curvy two-lane road that still bore patches of ice.

Krista gripped the wheel. The Subaru Boxer Engine howled, and she hazarded a glance at the dash. Forty-five in a twenty-five. Her lungs heaved. The Forester's tires screeched around a corner, and the force of the turn pushed Skip against the door.

"Take it easy," he said.

"I know what I'm doing."

But to be safe, she glanced at Skip to confirm he was wearing his seat belt. His eyes were glued to the road, and he gripped the door handle so hard his knuckles were white.

Gaines had a hundred-yard lead. She pushed her speed to fifty, but Gaines increased his lead through the next two miles of relatively straight roads. Hairpin turns were coming up. They passed Gumtree Road, Firtree Drive, and Elkwood Drive. Gaines came to a contractor's truck going the speed limit and passed it on the left. The truck pulled to a stop on the shoulder, and Krista sped by a few seconds later. After Chestnut Lane, they careened through a section of gentle curves. Krista held her breath as Gaines entered the hairpin turn at Fortunes Ridge.

"He's not going to make it," she yelled.

The Chrysler's rear tires began to slip but then caught the pavement again, and he finished the turn in the wrong lane.

Please. No oncoming traffic. Please.

They entered more sharp turns. Gaines was too far ahead to see. Krista braked hard to avoid an icy patch, then jammed on the gas. Her weight shifted left with the next turn, then hard to the right. At the next turn, there was more ice than she remembered. The right-hand wheels skidded off the road onto the shoulder, and Skip stared out the window at the ditch. They might roll. But then the all-wheel drive kicked in, and the left tires pulled them back onto the road.

"Slow down for chrissakes," yelled Skip.

"Relax. I've got it."

"You're going to get us killed."

"Don't be a wuss."

Nevertheless, she gave the accelerator a break through the next turn. The road straightened, and she could see Gaines again. There were only a few more turns to go. If he made it to Highway 664, he could use the Chrysler's bigger engine to press his lead. She hoped her colleagues had enough time to barricade the road. Thick ice made the last few turns treacherous, and Krista reduced her speed. She made it through the first turn, approached Headwaters Lane, and slammed on the brakes.

A skid mark ran across the road onto the ice. Gaines's car had slid on the ice and crashed nose-first into the guardrail on the right of Headwaters Lane. Krista pulled the Forester to a stop behind the Chrysler and flipped on her hazard lights. Skip was out the door in an instant, and she followed suit.

The Chrysler's front end was a mess. The engine hissed, and steam poured from under the hood. The airbags had deployed and now filled the front compartment. Skip yanked the driver's door open and reached inside to pull a stunned Gavin Gaines from the vehicle. Gaines had lost his cap in the commotion. He wavered on his feet, and Skip held his arm to keep him steady.

"Who the heck are you?" said Gaines.

Skip held out his badge. "Special Agent Edward Forrester of the FBI."

"The what?" said Gaines. He blinked erratically.

"Federal Bureau of Investigation. Maybe you've heard of us."

"Who the heck is she?" said Gaines.

"This is Special Officer Krista Jackson of the Wintergreen PD. She was driving."

Krista used her cell phone to call the office with an update. They needed a squad car and an EMS team to check Gaines out.

"Why are you guys hassling me?" said Gaines. "I was out for a drive."

Skip heaved a sigh. "Save it, dude. You're in a heap of trouble."

FORTY-FOUR

B ill had arranged to meet Elsie Dale at the Black Bear Creamery in Nellysford. The heiress was scouting property south of Charlottesville and agreed to come west a few miles for the interview. Bill had racked his brain for a suitable meeting place, then remembered the Black Bear, which served some of the best ice creams he'd ever tasted.

With a lot of luck, I might catch a killer and grab a tasty treat in one stop.

Now, that would be a first. Unfortunately for Bill, he forgot the creamery didn't open until noon, which left Mitch and him with nothing better to do than sit in the idling squad car. However, the owner must have seen them in the parking lot, because he came outside to ask if he could help.

"No, thanks," said Mitch through the open window. "We're waiting for somebody. Shouldn't take long. We'll try not to scare off any customers."

"You guys want to come inside while you wait?" The owner wore a white apron and a genuine smile. "Give you a free ice cream."

"Nah," said Mitch. "We're good."

Bill touched Mitch's arm. "Hold on there, Mitch. Have you ever had Black Bear's ice cream?"

Mitch shook his head.

"You're in for a treat."

Bill took his time selecting the right flavor for his waffle cone. The Rocky Road tempted him, but he finally settled on the mint chocolate chip. Mitch opted for the gingersnap. Since they were already there, Bill picked up a pint of hand-packed vanilla as well. Despite the owner's offer, Bill insisted on paying for everything and threw two bucks in the tip jar to get the party started.

Once outside, Mitch took a monster lick of his gingersnap, then nodded at the pint container Bill held. "That ice cream is going to melt in the cruiser."

"Not if we wait out here."

"Jeez, Bill. It can't be more than forty degrees."

"We won't have to wait long. Here Ms. Dale is now."

A high-end BMW rolled to a stop in the lot, and Elsie Dale exited the passenger side. She marched onto the wooden deck where they stood, none too happy by her expression.

"Nice place to meet," she said after scrutinizing the creamery's façade. "But I guess Nellysford is short on coffee houses."

"Can I tempt you with a morning ice cream?" said Bill.

Elsie Dale frowned.

"Are you sure? They're super good."

"No. Thank you."

Bill had found over the years that he generally admired wealthy people who made their own money, but those who inherited their riches often rubbed him the wrong way. Elsie Dale matched that paradigm well.

"We could have met at the IGA," he said, "but that would not have allowed much privacy."

Elsie hmpfed.

"There's always the squad car," said Mitch.

Elise Dale shook her head and marched to the nearest picnic table. "I can't imagine this will take long. I've already told you everything I know about this murder."

But Bill knew that was a lie, and after they all sat, he had Mitch explain that the time stamp on Elsie's gas purchase was ninety minutes earlier than she had indicated in her statement.

Dale lowered her eyebrows, and vertical lines formed on her forehead. She had a beautiful face, except when she frowned, which was often.

"Are you sure?" she said.

"Yes, ma'am," said Mitch.

"I must have gotten on the road earlier than I remembered."

"Early enough to arrive in Wintergreen before Ms. Key was killed," said Bill.

"What are you implying?"

Instead of answering, Bill attended to his morning dessert. The silky texture of the cream was a perfect complement to the crunchy chocolate chips. The advantage of eating ice cream outside in winter was that it melted much slower than in the summer months.

He now believed Dale had the strongest motive of all the likely suspects. Jealousy. It must have driven her crazy to know Kent was sleeping with Cassandra on the sly.

Bill said, "A few moments ago, you claimed you had already shared everything you know. But that isn't true, is it?"

"Of course it's true."

"No, it isn't. You lied about when you left Chesapeake on the day Ms. Key was killed. You left much earlier."

"That was a simple mistake."

"Are you sure there isn't something else?"

"I'm growing weary of this idiotic conversation. There *is* nothing else."

"Then I regret to inform you that your fiancé was having a clandestine affair with Cassandra Key."

Bill observed Dale's expression. A pink color rose to her cheeks, and her eyes burned, but there was no hint of surprise. Only anger.

"You already knew that," said Bill. "You knew that Kent couldn't resist her. That must have burned you up. With all your money, beauty, and power, you still couldn't keep him from nestling up to Cassandra whenever she called. So, you decided to change the landscape to your advantage, like you have many times before."

"No," said Elsie Dale.

"You hired a professional killer, then drove here early in the morning. I'm not sure how you knew Cassandra would go hiking, but you did. You spotted her hiking and radioed her position to Frank Richardi. He did the rest."

"This is utter BS."

"Is it?" said Bill. "All of it?"

Dale fiddled with her engagement ring, a large diamond in an oval cut. Her eyes moved from Bill to Mitch, and her lower teeth bit her upper lip.

"Oh, for the love of Queen Mary, yes, I knew Kent was cheating on me with Cassandra. I pay people to know everything about everyone around me. Clearly, I overestimated Kent's character. He brings positive attributes to the deal. He's easy to look at, and the State Department career reads well. But infidelity before marriage? That sort of behavior makes for tabloid headlines. Kent has to go, and I've known that for weeks now."

Bill pursed his lips. Perhaps he had misread the situation.

"But murder Cassandra Key?" said Dale. "No chance.

Except for her connection with Kent, I would scarcely have noticed her. She ran a small retail chain—for Pete's sake—and barely kept it afloat. I might have taken revenge if Cassandra had lived long enough, but that would have come in the business world. I could have swatted her around like a cat does a mouse. Murdering her would have only put me at risk. I would never kill anyone for love. Marriage is for convenience, sex, and power. Perhaps even procreation. If it doesn't work out, there's always divorce, provided you have the right prenuptial agreement. And I have great lawyers."

After Dale had left, Bill ate his ice cream out of obligation more than anything. He hardly noticed the flavor.

"Do you believe she's guilty?" said Mitch.

"Hmm."

"That wasn't a confident response."

"What's your view?" said Bill.

"She's ruthless, but her arguments were logical. She wouldn't take that kind of risk."

"Yeah." Bill munched on the last bit of his waffle cone. After swallowing, he said, "Maybe it wasn't any of these guys. Maybe Richardi acted alone."

Mitch shook his head. "No, that's not right. At a minimum, somebody delivered the sniper drone. And, as you've already guessed, I think someone radioed Key's location and description to Richardi."

Bill kept his own counsel. In a short period, Mitch had matured as a cop. He would make a fine detective someday, if he ever got the chance. But Wintergreen was a small shop for that.

On the way out of the lot, Bill's cell phone buzzed. It was Emily Powell. After updating Bill on Krista and Skip's car chase, Emily shared more news. They had finally located

Allen Steele, the fourth board member. He had returned home to a senior living facility in Richmond.

"Is he up for a visit?" asked Bill.

"Most definitely," said Emily. "And get this—he says he knows who killed Cassandra Key."

FORTY-FIVE

Mitch and Bill barreled east on Interstate 64 through the hills west of Charlottesville. Hardwood forests lined the road, and a tall fence kept deer from wandering into harm's way. Only a few patches of snow remained from the earlier storm, but a new front promised more precipitation that night.

Bill hardly noticed his surroundings. He agreed with Mitch's assessment of Elsie Dale. She was a cunning heiress with a plan and would never allow frivolous emotions to distract her. Dealing with an unfaithful fiancé was only slightly more inconvenient than a broken heel. Time for a new pair of shoes. And Cassandra Key? Completely irrelevant.

Which left Bill with Kent Olsen and Bryan McCasland. Sheesh. What a choice. A weak-willed junior diplomat versus a drone pilot turned back-office bureaucrat. What was Bill to believe? One of these guys had paid Frank Richardi hundreds of thousands of dollars to commit the perfect murder? Bill grimaced. But who else was there? Nikki Churchill? The soft-spoken assistant who had reported her boss missing and then joined the rescue effort to find her? Bill pressed the heel of his hand against his eye. He felt no closer to understanding the murder than he had on day one. But Allen Steele—the missing and infirm trustee—offered new hope. Early on, Bill concluded that Frank Richardi had help from someone on the mountain, so Bill searched for the motive there. Perhaps Steele would provide a new motive. A new suspect.

Bill's hands tingled. He loved this part of detective work the most. The possibility of finding a vital clue around the next corner. The critical puzzle piece that, once in place, would allow everything else to come together. He willed Mitch to drive faster. They still had an hour to go.

They passed the first Charlottesville exit, and Mitch took an extra moment to gaze in the city's direction.

"The Charlottesville PD wants to interview me," Mitch said.

What?

Bill's mind snapped back to the here and now.

"Okay," he said.

"I'm trying to figure out what to do."

Mitch shared what was going through his mind. Lulu would soon start dental school in Richmond, and they planned to move to Charlottesville to split their commute times. His drive from Charlottesville to Wintergreen would take an hour, which was manageable. But of course, the downtown police station was much closer, and they had open positions. Working for a bigger department meant more money and opportunities, but Mitch owed a loyalty obligation to Wintergreen. When he had wanted to move back to the area, Wintergreen had been the only police department to offer him a job.

"How long have you worked for Wintergreen PD?" asked Bill.

"Three years and change."

"They've gotten their money's worth, so don't worry about that."

"So, I should go for it?"

Bill scrutinized Mitch's face. He was in his late twenties and at the beginning of his career. For selfish reasons, Bill hoped Mitch would stay with Wintergreen. As a resident, Bill wanted a strong community police department, and Mitch was a good cop. Also, he considered Mitch a friend. But Mitch had asked for his advice, so Bill had to examine the question from Mitch's perspective.

"You should do the interview. There's little downside in that, and you'll learn from the experience in any case."

Mitch said, "Makes sense."

"Now, whether you accept an offer to work for them is a different matter. Make no mistake, this is a big decision with significant consequences for your career. And only you can make the decision, because your career is more important to you than anyone else."

"You stayed with the Columbia PD for thirty years, right? You must have had opportunities elsewhere. Why did you stay on?"

Bill smiled. At the age of thirty-five, he'd had an opportunity to take a role in Atlanta. More money. More upside. But his boys were little then, and he and Wanda were happy. They had recently moved into a new home.

"Columbia worked for me," said Bill. "It's the state capital and the second largest city in South Carolina, so it's kind of a big deal. Columbia also has many more citizens than Charlottesville by a wide margin, but Charlottesville is growing. I imagine there'll be good opportunities over the next twenty years."

Mitch eyed the road ahead. His face was tense, and he

gripped the steering wheel tightly. "Yeah," he said. "It's a big decision."

Bill figured Mitch had to leave Wintergreen at some point. He'd want the money and experience that a larger department provided. Bill knew from earlier conversations that Mitch and Lulu planned on having a family, which meant money would also be a factor. But the experience was even more critical. Mitch had learned much of what he could as a patrol officer for Wintergreen. To feel good about his career and himself, Mitch needed to set higher goals and accomplish more significant objectives.

"Take the interview," said Bill. "The decision will be easier to make once you have more data."

"Thanks. I'll do that."

FORTY-SIX

An hour later, a contrite Gavin Gaines had a bruise on the right side of his face from the airbag. The EMS team had cleared him, and he now sat in the conference room with Emily, Skip, and Krista.

He looks like a human weasel, Krista thought, *with that narrow face and pointy chin. Probably why he grew the mustache.*

Emily had called Arnie Shields at the sheriff's office with an update, but Arnie couldn't make it. They had a special operation underway and needed to focus on that. Arnie promised to dispense a deputy to pick Gaines up when he could. Meanwhile, Emily should proceed as she saw fit.

Emily sat at the end of the table. She wore a mean expression. Emily was a mild-mannered deputy chief and smiled at nearly everyone, but she took her job seriously. Nothing got under her skin like someone endangering the Wintergreen community.

"Mr. Gaines, you have committed a long list of offenses today," said Emily. "And we will have you in our custody for quite some time."

"What offenses? Speeding?"

"Yes, speeding. But also reckless driving and reckless endangerment. And that's only the start of the list. Wait until the commonwealth attorney goes to work."

"I think I want a lawyer."

Emily nodded to affirm that Gaines had made a reasonable point. "Here's how I see it. Listen carefully. If you murdered Cassandra Koy, you should hire a lawyer and not say a word to us until you do."

Gaines, who until that moment had adopted a why-are-you-cops-hassling-me demeanor, now grew tense. His eyes shifted to Skip.

"Don't look at him," said Emily. "He's with the FBI. He's no friend of yours."

"I didn't murder anybody," said Gaines.

"That's good," said Emily in an exaggerated tone. "Every morning, I tell my husband when he goes to work, 'Honey, try not to murder anyone today.'"

Gaines's eyebrows furrowed as if he couldn't follow Emily's point. Sarcasm was lost on him. It occurred to Krista that Gaines might be of only average intelligence.

"But here's the deal, Mr. Gaines," said Emily. She put her forefinger in the air. "You did something bad. Otherwise, you wouldn't have run when these guys approached your condo. Right?"

Despite Emily's earlier warning, Gaines's eyes circled the table, perhaps searching for a friendly face. He certainly didn't get one from Skip. Skip's jaw was set, and his dark eyes emanated fury.

I'm glad Skip's on our side, thought Krista.

Emily said, "I want to believe you, Mr. Gaines, and I could see my way to reducing those charges I mentioned earlier to just the speeding ticket. But to do that, I need you to tell me exactly what you did with that drone. Now, don't look surprised. We know you have a killer drone."

Krista frowned. What did Emily hope to accomplish by bringing up the killer drone? Surely, Gaines would demand a lawyer now. That's what Krista would do if she were in his position. Then again, for Gaines to request a lawyer, he had to admit to himself that he was bound to spend time behind bars, at least a day or two. On the other hand, if Gaines played Emily's game, he might believe he could get away with nothing more than a speeding ticket. But Gaines was more intelligent than he appeared.

"I definitely want a lawyer now."

Emily sighed and dropped her hands into her lap as if there was nothing more she could do.

Then Skip leaned forward. "Okay, Mr. Gaines. We all know you're in for much weightier charges than reckless driving. You're in line for accessory to murder here in Nelson County."

"I didn't murder anyone," said Gaines again, as if mere words could remove suspicion.

Skip shrugged. "We'll let the commonwealth attorney sort out the charges. But I'm willing to bet that you worked with your Army pal Oscar Yates to take a sniper drone out of inventory and deliver it to Frank Richardi."

"I don't know any Frank Richardi."

"But you know Oscar Yates, and you delivered the drone to someone on the day of Ms. Key's death."

"Says who?"

"We have a witness who saw you park a trailer in a strip mall in Charlottesville. You had coffee at Bonnie's Breakfast Place."

Gaines's face sagged.

"You've broken federal laws," said Skip, "but we'll deal with that later. Whether I help you out depends on what you tell us right now about where and to whom you delivered that drone."

"How are you going to help me?" Gaines said to Skip.

"That depends on what else you've done."

"Maybe I should hire a lawyer first, get this in writing."

"Fine with me," said Skip. "But that will take a day or two. We need your help now. We may not need it then."

For some reason, Gaines chose that moment to gaze at Krista, perhaps because both Emily and Skip have given him a hard time. Krista raised her eyebrows to acknowledge that he was in a tough spot. Gaines wiped a hand all around his weasel face.

"I was contacted anonymously over a year ago. December of last year."

"Anonymously?" said Skip.

Gaines shrugged. "A lot of stuff gets done anonymously on the dark web. Anyway, the potential client said they wanted to test drive a sniper drone. I figured they were an arms dealer for another country. An Israeli company was manufacturing the drones, and I knew the Army had already procured some."

"And you knew how to get one of these drones?" said Skip.

Gaines stared at Skip with dead eyes. His lips were a flat line. Krista feared that Gaines had spoken his last word.

Skip may have had the same concern, because he said, "Forget I asked that question. Please proceed."

"Everything I say from here on is hypothetical," said Gaines. "Understand?"

"No," said Skip. "What's that mean?"

"It means I'm telling you a fictional story. In a galaxy far away, this could have happened."

Skip rolled his eyes. "Okay. Let's hear it."

Gaines continued. "In this other world, I knew a guy who knew a guy who could get anything from the Army, particularly on a short-term basis. This alien client was prepared to pay handsomely and in bitcoin."

"How much bitcoin?" said Skip.

"Hypothetically?"

"Of course."

"Three."

Krista bit her lip and tried to keep up. The alien client had to be Frank Richardi. But what were three bitcoins worth in dollars? Judging by Emily's expression, she had the same question. Skip helped them out.

"What are three bitcoins worth these days?" he said. "Seventy thousand or so?"

"Almost seventy-six," said Gaines.

"Sweet," said Skip. "What did you have to do to earn three bitcoins in this alternate universe?"

"Galaxy," said Gaines. "Faraway galaxy. I don't believe in that multiverse nonsense."

Skip's expression seemed to say he wasn't sure solving Cassandra Key's murder was worth putting up with this childish game. But he must have decided to stick it out.

"I stand corrected," Skip said. "Faraway galaxy."

"The alien client said they would specify the where, when, and how. We were all set to go twice before—six months back and three months back—but the client canceled both times. The waiting was stressful, but the client had paid one bitcoin up front, so I put up with the hassle. Then I got word on the timing of delivery and a special request. The client wanted me to get involved with the drone show up here in case anything went wrong with the test flight. I told them nothing would go wrong, but they insisted. I didn't feel good about that, and I was right. Look where it got me."

"How did you get the drone company to hire you?" said Skip. "Is Chas Skibinski involved?"

"No. I planned to come up and hung around for a week before the show, but then I found out the production company had an opening for a freelance pilot. I'm certified, so that was easy."

"Describe the hypothetical delivery," said Emily.

"Not much to it. I picked up a truck and trailer near Fort Belvoir. The drone was on the back, covered with a tarp. I drove the truck to Charlottesville and left it in a parking lot with the keys under the floor mat. I killed five hours drinking coffee and slogging around the strip center. Then I drove the trailer back to Fort Belvoir."

"Who picked up the trailer in Charlottesville?" asked Emily.

"I don't know. The client told me to leave the trailer in the lot, kill some time, and come back five hours later."

"Are you sure you didn't see who picked it up?" said Skip. "Maybe you watched from across the mall."

"No. The client was clear on that."

"Did you inspect the drone?"

"Yes. I pulled into a gas station to take a peek. Pretty slick, hypothetically speaking."

"What else can you tell us?" said Emily.

Gaines claimed he had told them everything he knew. Emily left Gaines in the conference room, asked a patrol officer to watch the door, and then she and Skip and Krista conferred in the chief's office.

Emily lifted both hands to massage her temples. "Okay, Skip, how do you read this clown?"

Skip rubbed his hands together as if he savored his position. "Gaines is connected with the theft and sale of Army weapons and ammunition on the black market. We will come down on him and his buddies like an avalanche."

"That's great for you," said Emily. "But what about our case?"

"Oh. Yeah." Skip paused to switch gears. "Richardi carefully constructed his plan. He required the use of a drone so he could kill Key remotely and get away clean even if things went wrong. He wanted to do it where other drones were operating to provide him with cover. He timed it to coincide with a meeting of the Old Virginia Gun Club because that would naturally provide other likely suspects."

Emily crossed her arms. "But how did he know the drone guys and Key's club would be here at the same time?"

Skip frowned, unsure. Emily asked Krista for her thoughts.

"Maybe Richardi got lucky," said Krista.

"Luck?" said Emily. "I'm not a big fan of luck as a logical explanation."

Krista said, "What I mean is perhaps Richardi had found a way to hack into Cassandra Key's calendar. When he learned Key planned to come to Wintergreen, he researched the resort and learned about the drone show. Then he contacted Gaines."

Emily nodded and said, "So, you believe Richardi acted alone?"

"I don't know," said Krista. "Maybe."

But upon considering Emily's question further, Krista doubted her own answer. Even if Richardi had seen Cassan-

229

dra's calendar, how did he know where to find Cassandra that morning?

Krista said, "Maybe we should give Mitch and Bill an update and see what they think."

"Good idea," said Emily. "Let's get them on the phone."

FORTY-SEVEN

James River Meadows was a senior living facility in the western suburbs of Richmond. Out front, white columns supported a portico over the entrance and circular driveway. The flowerbeds were cut back for the winter, but numerous boxwoods provided ample greenery to cheer up the single-story brick building's façade.

Once inside the lobby, Bill explained to the front desk attendant that Mr. Steele was expecting their visit. She asked them to sign in and gave directions to room 137.

In a nicely decorated sitting room to the left, several older women quietly focused their attention on a jigsaw puzzle. Three elderly gentlemen sat on a couch in the lobby and watched Bill and Mitch's every move. They wore dress pants and sweaters. One of them held a cane between his legs. A high-end walker with wheels, handbrakes, and a seat stood to one side.

"How y'all doing?" said Mitch.

Two men smiled instantly and returned Mitch's greeting. The third man didn't respond, and Bill guessed he might be hard of hearing.

The building had two wings of about twenty rooms each. They took the left wing and found Room 137 near the end of the hallway.

A woman in her early sixties with white curly hair answered the door and introduced herself as Steele's daughter, Ellen Long. The apartment consisted of a living room with a small bedroom and bathroom through doorways on the right. Ellen Long invited them inside, where they met Allen Steele, who sat in a comfortable armchair with a blanket draped over his legs. A cane was hooked onto the back of his chair. The side table next to him supported a stack of hardback books.

After introductions, Allen Steele regarded Mitch in his uniform. Mitch was still standing and had great posture.

"How old are you?" said Steele.

"Twenty-eight."

"You look good in that uniform," Steele said. "I looked almost that good in my Army uniform a million years ago."

"Almost," said Mitch, "but not quite."

Which set Steele and his daughter both to howling. Bill noticed they had similar facial features with kind eyes and large noses.

Ellen offered Bill and Mitch something to drink. She had water, coffee, or herbal tea.

"We also have wine," said Steele, hopefully.

Ellen frowned.

"What?" he said. "It's afternoon."

"These gentlemen are working," she said.

Allen gave Ellen the side-eye but accepted her point. Mitch asked for water, and Allen and Bill opted for coffee.

Once they were settled with drinks, Allen Steele leaned forward and said, "I expect you want to know who's responsible for Cassandra Key's murder."

"Very much so," said Bill.

"I won't beat around the bush. It was a man named Lorenzo Conti."

Bill glanced at Ellen to gauge her reaction. She raised an eyebrow slightly but displayed no other physical response. She might have heard this revelation from her father before, perhaps many times.

"Please proceed," said Bill. "We'll pay close attention."

Then, Steele told them a strange account of events that had transpired three years earlier. Cassandra had become president the year before. Steele had preceded her in the role for fifteen years and was to remain on the board as a trustee emeritus indefinitely.

"We all knew the story," said Steele. "The Old Virginia Gun Club was in a long, slow decline. Frankly, the transition from me to Cassandra was rocky. In retrospect, I should have left sooner, but I didn't want to."

"You were a great leader for many years," said Ellen, as if to reassure her father.

Allen nodded. "For a while, yes, but I wasn't the right person for the future. We lost a lot of members during my last few years, and the trend continued with Cassandra as president. Frankly, I'd given up. I believed our best course was to restructure into a smaller enterprise, but then Lorenzo Conti showed up."

"Who is Lorenzo Conti?" said Bill.

Allen Steele squinted at Bill. "Are you really in law enforcement?"

Mitch said, "Bill's from South Carolina. He moved to Virginia six months ago."

Steele nodded to show he now understood Bill's ignorance. "Conti was the closest thing to organized crime we ever had in southeast Virginia. For decades, he had his fingers in illegal businesses that catered to illegal tastes in Norfolk, Virginia Beach, and the surrounding areas. I never met the man myself and was shocked when one of his underlings showed up at my office, claiming that Conti wanted to join the OVGC. Apparently, they thought I was still the president. The story was that the aging Conti wished to polish his legacy by joining a few classy organizations. The underling implied that Conti would make a sizable donation above the initiation fee. I told the guy I had stepped down but would pass the message on to the new president."

Hairs on the back of Bill's neck tingled. According to Skip's FBI report, during his active period, Frank Richardi often worked for organized crime.

Steele paused for a sip of coffee and then continued his story. "I took Conti's request to Cassandra, and she rejected it immediately. She got huffy about it. How dare a lowlife like Conti propose such a thing?"

"How did Conti react to being rejected?" said Mitch.

"Before I could communicate the message, Conti's underling returned to my office with another proposal. Apparently, they had now researched Cassandra and knew she owned a chain of gun stores."

Bill leaned forward and rubbed his hands together. Intuition told him Steele's story was about to get a lot more interesting.

Steele's eyes grew big, and he said, "Get this. Conti wanted to buy guns in bulk from Cassandra's business at retail prices. For every gun he purchased, he would donate a hundred dollars to the OVGC. He wanted to buy a lot of guns. Thousands of guns." Steele shook his head. "Of course, I knew Conti planned to sell the guns on the black market. He'd probably end up shipping most of them to Mexico and other countries. I was absolutely terrified. I was a corporate lawyer for darn near fifty years, and that was the closest I ever came to organized crime."

"What did Cassandra say?" asked Bill.

"The strangest thing," said Steele. "I expected her to reject the proposal like before, and I had no idea what we would do then. But she didn't. I'll remember that conversation forever. We were on the phone, and she paused for a long time before giving me a non-answer. Cassandra asked for the underling's number and said she would contact him."

Bill grimaced. He could guess how the story ended.

Steele wrung his hands and stared at the floor. His daughter reached to touch his shoulder, and he nodded. "I found out later that Cassandra worked with the state police to stage a sting operation. They eventually arrested three guys, including the underling who had contacted me. But as you might expect, nothing tied back to Conti himself." Steele took a deep breath. "You should never cross a criminal like Conti. I told Cassandra I feared for her life, but she laughed that off. According to her, Conti wouldn't do anything because the police had eyes on him."

Mitch said, "Do you believe this man Conti arranged to have her killed after all these years?"

"No," said Steele.

Bill pulled back, surprised.

Steele said, "A couple of years ago, a pal told me Conti had suffered a bad stroke and would never recover. But crime families have long memories. I think someone connected to Conti did it."

Revenge, thought Bill, *is the best motive we've heard yet for this thing.*

Cassandra Key had lived her life her way, not caring two hoots for what others thought or felt. But when she crossed organized crime, she went too far. And she died for it, died in the snow, murdered in white.

≈

Sitting at a nearby fast-food restaurant, Bill called Krista and asked her to try to locate Lorenzo Conti. She called back in five minutes.

"He's in an assisted living place in Newport News."

Krista gave Bill the number, and then Bill asked her to search for a connection between any of their suspects and the Conti family.

"Add Gavin Gaines to the list," he said, "and anyone else close to this."

"What about Chas Skibinski?" said Mitch.

"Yeah. Good call."

When Krista hung up, Bill called the Newport News facility to request a visit with Conti. After Bill made his pitch, the woman who answered the phone put him on hold. He waited a full minute, and then another woman picked up.

Bill restated his request, and the woman said, "I'm sorry. That won't be possible."

"I only need a few minutes of his time. I can be there in an hour."

"He's in a memory unit, sir. There's no point."

Had Conti actually suffered a stroke? Was he in a memory unit? Or was it a ruse that allowed the old man to escape the prying eyes of the law?

"This is police business," he said. "I'm with the Wintergreen PD."

"You could be with Homeland Security, and the answer would be the same. The family has left strict instructions."

The woman then informed Bill that additional questions should be addressed to a specific attorney at a particular firm.

"No luck?" said Mitch, after Bill ended the call.

Bill shook his head.

"What now?" said Mitch.

"Now, we drive west and call Emily."

FORTY-EIGHT

In the Wintergreen PD conference room, the discussion went around the table for ninety minutes. Bill, Mitch, Krista, Emily, and Skip Forrester each had an opinion about whether another party had helped Frank Richardi kill Cassandra Key. Emily thought no. They had already solved the case. The Conti family hired Richardi, and Gavin Gaines delivered the trailer to Richardi in Charlottesville. Somehow, Richardi figured out how to find Cassandra Key on the mountain by himself.

Emily had bags under her eyes and walked with stooped shoulders. Managing a case like this took a heavy toll, and with three young kids at home, she badly needed a break. Had weariness contributed to Emily's conclusion that they were at an end?

An hour into the meeting, Skip Forrester received a call confirming that the FBI believed Richardi had worked for the Conti organization on previous assignments. It was evident that Conti's thirst for revenge ultimately spelled Key's demise. Unfortunately, though Krista had spent hours online, she still hadn't found a connection between one of their suspects and the Conti family.

Bill—who had spent the two-hour ride from Richmond silently rehashing the interviews he'd done—was convinced he had missed something. But spending more time pushing the data around the conference table would not help. Like Emily, Bill needed a break.

Emily suggested they suspend the discussion, go their separate ways for dinner to give their minds a rest, and then regroup on a video call later that night. Everyone welcomed the change, particularly Bill, because he badly wanted to take Curly out before Frieda Chang returned at seven o'clock.

Outside, without the sun's warmth, the temperature had quickly dropped into the twenties. Bill cranked the heat in his Mazda and began the curvy drive up the mountain. Heavy snowflakes fell through his headlight beams. To take his mind off the case, Bill switched on the radio, even though Wintergreen's reception was iffy at best. The first clear station he found played a catchy Latin pop song that Bill enjoyed to the end. When the host began addressing her audience in Spanish, Bill reached to change the station.

Wait.

The Mazda approached an overlook, and Bill pulled into the parking lot.

Oh.

A sinking feeling entered Bill's chest. He examined the puzzle from a new angle, and more pieces fell into place.

He called Krista. Was she still at the office? Yes. Could she check something specific? Yes.

Bill drove the rest of the way to his condo, parked, and hoped Krista would prove him wrong. He didn't want to believe that Nikki Churchill was guilty, even though he knew it was true.

The Conti family had hired Frank Richardi—their faithful contractor—to come out of retirement long enough to kill Cassandra Key. After careful planning, Frank rented a killer drone from Gavin Gaines and instructed him to bring it to Charlottesville. Frank picked up the drone and drove it to the top of Old Stoney Creek Road. Once there, Frank launched the drone and directed it remotely through its short and deadly flight. From somewhere in Wintergreen, Nikki gave Frank directions on how to find Cassandra. Bill could only guess at how Nikki trailed Cassandra that morning. She may have dropped Cassandra off at the trailhead. Or they may have discussed Cassandra's route the night before, which would have made it easy for Nikki to follow her.

Bill's phone buzzed. Krista.

"You were right," she said. "Nikki passed the criminal background check, but I can't find much on her before she began working for Cassandra three years ago. No old addresses. No social media. What should I do now?"

"Call Emily. She'll want to meet. I'm not sure where Nikki is now. She might have left the mountain already. I must take Curly for a walk and meet Frieda. Then I'll return to the station."

Once inside the condo, Bill pulled Curly's harness on, and then his phone buzzed again, a text from Frieda.

Home soon. Passing Wintergreen entrance now.

Bill replied with a thumbs up. Good. He had enough time to take Curly for a quick tour around the condo building. Curly ran up and down the hall, excited about something.

"You know your mommy's coming, don't you?" said Bill.

As if to answer, Curly wagged his tail and scampered to the door. Outside, they descended the stairwell and walked back to the slope's edge. Down at the Mountain Inn, spotlights illuminated the trails for night skiing. The wind had calmed, and light snow fell. Snowmaking machines churned loudly on the nearby Highland Express runs. Across the hollow, lighted homes along Blackrock Drive made for a cheery sight. The comforting scent of home fires lingered in the air. Bill scanned the dark balconies in the condo building behind him. Everyone had pulled their window coverings closed for the night.

It was his first winter in the mountains, and despite the near constant chill and the short days, he had to admit that even the coldest season brought its own special magic to Wintergreen. Still, after this most recent snowstorm, a quick trip to Florida would make for a nice break. He wondered whether Cindy might come along. It was certainly worth asking.

"Beautiful, isn't it?" said a woman.

Bill startled. A dark form stood six feet away.

"Nikki!"

Nikki Churchill wore black pants, a black top, and a black cap. Even her sling was dark, as if she wished to blend with the night.

"Surprised to see me?" she said.

"Um. Yeah, I guess."

"I was heading back to Norfolk and stopped by to thank you for all the help."

Another long pause. Too long.

Say something.

"Okay," said Bill. "Sure."

"You don't seem happy that I'm here."

Curly, who had initially wagged his tail upon seeing Nikki, now growled at the threatening tone of her voice.

Nikki's left arm hung by her side, and she carried something in her hand.

Bill realized she had a gun. He grew weak in the knees.

Curly barked once.

Nikki pointed her weapon at the dog.

"Shut him up quick, Bill."

Bill scooped Curly into his arms. The dog squirmed to be free. Curly barked again, and Nikki pointed the gun at Bill's face. His heart rate jumped.

"Don't do that," said Bill. "Take it easy. I'll calm him down in a second."

"You'd better."

Bill stroked Curly gently and spoke to him in a comforting tone. The poodle soon relaxed, and Nikki lowered her weapon.

"You've got it all figured out anyway, haven't you?" she said.

"I'm afraid so. The Wintergreen PD is searching for you now. Give me the gun, and I'll drive you to the station."

Nikki chuckled. "Now, why would I do that?"

She asked the question in a tone that suggested Bill had little chance of convincing her to change course.

"Why are you here?" he said.

"I had to find out. The family told me you called the assisted living facility, and I thought you were getting close. How did you know it was me?"

Breathe. Breathe. Stay calm.

Bill had been in tense situations before. Talking was good. Anything that kept her from pulling the trigger was good.

"You don't speak Spanish," he said. "When we first met,

242

you told me your mother was Mexican to explain your complexion. But you couldn't speak a word of Spanish with the housekeeper from Guatemala. Your ancestors are Italian. I'd guess you're related to Lorenzo Conti, maybe a grand-daughter."

"A distant cousin. They wouldn't risk a direct-line family member on a three-year gig like this."

"Is your real name Nikki?"

"Yeah. Nicole, actually, but I go by Nikki. An assumed identity works better if you keep your first name. Of course, I'm not a Churchill."

What would Nikki do now that she knew the police would soon be after her? She didn't seem anxious or panicked, which worried Bill. She held the gun naturally. That was also bad.

"Nikki, if you shoot me now, five neighbors will call it in. You'll never escape."

"I'm not an amateur. There's a silencer on this gun. And anyway, I'm not going to shoot you."

"Good. Good. I'll give you an hour's head start. Once you're off the mountain, there are many different ways out of here."

Nikki snickered. "What? I should trust you?"

"Yes. I promise."

"Is that a cross-your-heart-and-hope-to-die promise?"

She was making fun of him now.

"Turn around, Bill," she said. "I'll give you a little tap on the head, and you'll nap for thirty minutes. That's all I need."

Bill detected movement at the side of the building. He told himself to stand still.

"I don't want to turn around," he said.

Nikki raised the pistol again.

Bill's mind was blank.

Think. Think.

"Answer a couple of questions for me?" he said.

"What difference does it make?"

"It'll ease my mind."

"Two questions. Go."

"Why didn't they use you instead of Frank Richardi?"

Nikki shook her head. "Idiots. I offered to do the job, but someone wanted to use Mr. Reliable. Then Frank got himself caught, which ruined everything. How hard was it for him to drive to Dulles and get on a plane? If he hadn't screwed that up, you'd still be trying to figure out how Kent or Bryan made the shot."

Of course, she was right. Richardi's discovery had been the key break in the case.

"What was your original assignment?" said Bill.

"Get hired by Cassandra and provide intel for Frank. We could have done it years ago, but Frank became obsessed with using a killer drone. He insisted on it—claimed it was foolproof. I have to admit the tech is awesome. It might change everything."

There was definitely someone in the dark about twenty feet behind Nikki. A tall person.

Nikki said, "My job became finding a location and time when Cassandra would be in the vicinity of other drones. Frank said that would provide more cover. But it was hard to do. I had it lined up twice, and then she changed her schedule."

"You moved the retreat back a week."

"Yep. I fooled everyone into believing it was someone else's idea."

"And you rented that condo for Kent Olsen to finger him as the killer."

"You have to admit that was good."

Bill's mind froze. He couldn't come up with another question because the puzzle was complete. They had killed Cassandra in the morning. Nikki had time to eat lunch at the Edge and still get to the Plunge by one thirty.

"Do you want to turn around, or should I shoot you?" she said.

"Wait. I have another question. Where were you when radioed directions to Richardi?"

Nikki scratched her temple with the pistol's barrel, then lowered it to point at Bill again.

"On the slope behind the High Ridge Place condos. With the leaves all gone, I could see Cassandra's orange coat. It was cold sitting through the storm, but the snow hid me well."

Someone tapped Nikki's right shoulder. With her pistol raised, Nikki swung in that direction, but a massive fist clobbered her. Nikki fell where she stood and didn't move again. Unconscious.

Bill lowered Curly to the ground and then reached for Nikki's pistol.

Curly ran to his mother, and Frieda Chang picked him up.

Bill's lungs heaved. It would take a while for his heart to settle.

"Jeez," he said, "I've never been this happy to see anybody."

"What the heck's going on here, Bill?" said Frieda.

Bill gave Frieda a quick summary of events. Then he stared at Nikki on the ground.

"That was a heck of a right cross," he said. "Mind if I ask you a question?"

"Sure," said Frieda.

"What did you do before you were a romance writer?"

"I taught school for three years but wasn't very good at it."

"And before that?"

Frieda laughed. "I was an amateur boxer once. I won a few tournaments."

"I'll bet you did."

FORTY-NINE

Bill stood at the top of the hill and regarded the long white chute. He felt dizzy, and his lungs worked overtime.

"Easy, Bill," said Cindy. "You can do this. Hop on and let go."

"I don't know. Maybe I should watch you first."

"Come on. You can do it."

"Ready, sir?" said the attendant.

Bill glanced at the young man, who wore a red jacket and appeared to be in his late teens. He had a scruffy beard, piercing blue eyes, and a wide smile.

Oh, what the heck.

Bill flopped his tube onto the snow and climbed aboard. The attendant gave him a good shove, and gravity took over.

And then he was flying.

Terror gripped his stomach. Wind buffeted Bill's hair, and the frozen air assaulted his face. The tube rubbed loudly against the packed snow.

The terror slid away from Bill, and he laughed as the tube raced toward the bottom of the chute. As he drew closer to the end, the ride grew bumpy, and Bill feared he would flip and be ground against the snow. But the track bottomed out, and the tube raced upward and then stopped.

Bill struggled to stand up, laughing harder than he had in years.

He pulled his tube to the side and watched Cindy's ride. She screamed most of the way down and was breathless at the end. She pulled her tube off the ramp, and the two fell into each other's arms, smiling and giggling like teenagers.

FIFTY

itch poured a cup of coffee, stood at the kitchen sink, and gazed out the window at the nearby mountains. Patches of snow from the last storm remained in the shadows. The sun had risen but had not yet crested the ridge to the east. The cloudless sky was powder blue. He would miss that view in Charlottesville. They had found a nice home to rent northwest of town with a yard and hardwood trees. But no mountain view. This was their last night in Augusta County, and most of their stuff was already gone.

"Good morning," said Lulu, shuffling into the kitchen in a robe and slippers. She stopped by Mitch's side, touched his arm, and kissed him. "I think I'll have cereal today."

"Sorry, babe. The cereal is packed and gone."

"Oh, that's right." Lulu knelt at a cabinet near the sink. "Then I'll have a smoothie."

"Sorry again. Packed and gone."

Lulu stood and folded her arms. "You got a bit overzealous with the packing yesterday. What are we supposed to eat?"

Mitch stepped to the refrigerator and opened the door to

reveal a clean and mostly empty space. "Don't be so quick to judge. I'm making French toast."

Lulu cocked an eyebrow. "French toast? Do we have syrup?"

"Uh-huh. We also have almond milk and grapefruit." He lifted his cup. "And coffee."

She stepped close to Mitch and draped her arms around his neck. "You think of everything."

Mitch and Lulu sat on stools at the counter with their empty plates before them. The kitchen table and chairs had gone the day before, and they needed to get working on the move soon, but for now, they would enjoy a second cup of coffee. They discussed their regret over leaving one home and their excitement at moving to the next. Lulu's classes would begin in a few days. She would have a long commute, which would inevitably reduce their time together, but pursuing any dream required long days.

"Have you decided what to do?" said Lulu.

Mitch had interviewed with a sergeant in the Charlottesville Police Department. The sergeant had seemed like a solid boss and had indicated a job offer was likely if Mitch wanted to pursue the process.

"I made a list of the Charlottesville PD benefits," said Mitch. "The top three were more money, a shorter commute, and more advancement opportunities."

Lulu nodded. "That's a compelling list. What does Wintergreen have that Charlottesville doesn't?"

"Well, scenery, for one."

"Definitely. Mountains and trees beat the heck out of buildings and parking lots."

Mitch had stared at the piece of paper for a long time, but the rest of the Wintergreen pros were mighty soft stuff. The community and his colleagues. The calculation wasn't much of a challenge. The job in Charlottesville would lead to higher pay now and higher pay in the long run. A no-brainer.

Not that Lulu was pushing him in that direction. Not at all. She had said he'd already made a sacrifice by selling the house he inherited to pay for her tuition and fees. They had enough money to make it without him taking a job he didn't want. But if a family was in their future—and they both wanted a family—then saving money would be a way of life for a long, long time. Money mattered.

"What about Emily?" said Lulu. "Is she going to make chief?"

"It looks like it," said Mitch. "Alex Sharp told me he's ready to step down as acting chief and feels Emily is more than qualified. She was hesitant to take the job with an infant in the house, but she and her husband seem to have sorted a way to make it work."

"You always said you could learn a lot from Emily."

"True."

"And you like the rest of the team. Krista, John Hill, and the others."

"Uh-huh."

Of course, there was more to it than his departmental colleagues. Mitch was a part of the larger Wintergreen community. He knew many residents and felt a responsibility for them. When an older man's SUV slid on an icy patch and veered into a ditch the day before, Mitch and John Hill managed to get the SUV on the road without calling a tow truck. Was it a life-threatening situation? No. But it made Mitch feel good anyway.

And then there was Bill O'Shea. Bill was retired and not

an official member of the department, but he always seemed to be around when they needed an extra hand.

"Of course, it's your decision," said Lulu, "but staying with Wintergreen appears to have many benefits. And the Charlottesville PD will always be there if you want to move later."

Lulu smiled, and Mitch knew she'd be okay with whatever he decided. His chest swelled. She had a beautiful smile.

Jeez, he thought. *How did I get so lucky?*

"I guess I will," he said.

"Will what?"

"Stay in Wintergreen. At least for a while."

FIFTY-ONE

K rista checked her makeup in the visor mirror and adjusted her lipstick. Then she stepped out of her Forester into the Orzo Kitchen and Wine Bar parking lot on Charlottesville's West Main Street. Her stomach fluttered. She took hesitant steps toward the restaurant and then noticed Skip standing off to one side.

"Hey, there you are," he said.

"Here I am."

They came together, hesitated momentarily, and then settled on shaking hands. She hoped he didn't detect the perspiration on her palm.

Krista had changed her mind over what to wear many times before settling on faded jeans, a white buttoned shirt, and a black-and-gray checkered coat. Her sons had sensed early on that something was up, and they quizzed her about it. Yes, she had a date. Don't give me a hard time. It's in Charlottesville. Yes, I might be a little late. Yes, you can stay up and watch movies until I get home.

She'd been surprised when Skip called after they wrapped

up the Key investigation. They had spent a few surprisingly easy minutes chatting, and then he got to the point. He was taking a trip to Charlottesville. Would she care to meet for dinner? Oh. Okay. Long pause to put it all together. Sure. That sounds fun.

The Orzo Kitchen and Wine Bar had exposed ceilings and a long wooden bar. Jazz music played softly from speakers mounted high on the walls. A faint scent of garlic lingered in the air.

Krista and Skip were seated at a two-top on the left. He ordered a martini. She opted for a glass of wine because she had to drive home.

Skip wore a black sweater that went well with his prematurely gray hair.

"Just to be clear," she said, "this is an actual date. Right?"

"I certainly hope so," he said, "but we can move in another direction if you like."

"No, that's fine. I just like to know what's happening."

Skip smiled and then reached for his water glass. His fingers trembled slightly.

"So," she said, "do you have a meeting or something?"

He swallowed, set the glass down, and brought his hands together. "No. I came to see you."

"You did? And you're driving back tonight?"

Skip shook his head. "I booked a hotel. It's a long drive back after a few drinks."

It certainly was. The drive from northern Virginia was a minimum of two hours each way. Krista hoped Skip didn't have the expectation that she would be visiting his hotel room. If he did, this would be their one and only date. But going by his conduct during dinner, she didn't get that impression. They discussed many topics. The Key investigation. Bill O'Shea. Northern Virginia. His career in the FBI. Her burgeoning career as a police officer. His short marriage. Her somewhat longer marriage and her two boys, Ashton and Trevor.

"I've been meaning to ask you about your name," she said. "When we apprehended Gavin Gaines, you identified yourself as Edward Forrester. How do you get from Edward to Skip?"

Skip laughed. "Oh, that. I grew up in Hampton, Virginia, and I used to go sailing as a kid. I got pretty good at it and won some competitions."

"I see," she said. "First Skipper. Then Skip."

"That's it."

The food was delicious. Skip had grilled sea bass, and Krista chose the mushroom pasta. Skip ordered a glass of wine with dinner. Krista wanted another drink but stuck with water instead. After the meal, he asked if she was up for a stroll down Main Street, and they continued their conversation.

She kept looking for the warning signs of a deal killer. But he wasn't a political nut job, and he didn't have any off-putting habits. On the contrary, he was intelligent, amusing, and listened to every word she said. They walked a mile east to the University of Virginia grounds, and when they reached the Rotunda steps, Skip paused and turned toward her.

"I'd like to see you again," he said.

Krista sighed. "How does this possibly work? We're a three-hour drive apart. I have two boys in middle school."

"One step at a time," he said. "I like driving."

"Whatever you might think, I'm not sleeping with you tonight."

Skip raised his hands. "I wouldn't expect you to."

Krista studied his face. She detected no deception there, only genuine affection. When he lowered his hands again, she took them in hers.

"Okay, Skip Forrester," she said. "One step at a time."

FIFTY-TWO

Bill answered the door to find Frieda Chang wearing a black dress, a white puffer coat, and heels that brought her height above six foot six. Next to Frieda stood a black man of medium size wearing a light-brown leather jacket and jeans. Bill had only a moment to take in their appearance because, at his feet, Curly demanded his attention.

The white poodle wagged his tail with reckless abandon, and Bill stooped to hold Curly's head in his hands.

Bill said, "I'm glad you could make it, Curly. The party can now officially begin."

"Are you sure he's not too much?" said Frieda. "Curly can be a handful."

"He'll be fine," said Bill. "In anticipation of his visit, I picked up a bed in Waynesboro to make him feel at home. It's next to the fireplace."

"You're spoiling him, Bill."

"I try."

Curly took off to greet other guests, and Frieda introduced Bill to her friend Rodney, a science fiction writer who lived in Richmond.

"Pleased to meet you," said Bill.

"Likewise."

"Do I detect an Australian accent?" said Bill.

"Can't shake it," said Rodney. "I was born in Brisbane but have lived in the States for nearly a decade."

"Excellent," said Bill, smiling. "We're now an international party. Drop your coats in the guest bedroom and come grab a drink."

Bill had invited a small group of friends over to watch the drone show from his balcony. Phyllis Spooner and Alex Sharp—the acting chief of police who had returned from Florida that morning—rounded out the group of six. Cindy had prepared an enticing charcuterie board with three kinds of cheese, Italian salami, cornichons, grapes, nuts, pepper jelly, and an assortment of crackers. Bill served wine and cocktails.

At the counter next to the refrigerator, Bill measured ingredients into a shaker for French 75s: gin, lemon juice, simple syrup, and lots of ice. Bill shook the shaker, and the ice quickly chilled the liquid inside. Bill poured the mixture into three champagne flutes, and Alex Sharp strolled up.

"Sorry all that stuff happened when I was away," Alex said.

"No problem," said Bill. "Emily did a fine job in your place."

Bill lifted an open bottle and carefully added three ounces of champagne to each flute.

"There's a bit of news on that front," said Alex. "I told the board I want to go back to selling real estate and that they need to promote Emily into the chief's slot."

"What did they say?"

"They approved it unanimously."

"Good call."

Bill put a lemon twist into each of the glasses and then handed one to Alex.

"You deserve a mini-celebration," said Bill. "You were an excellent acting chief."

Alex shook his head. "You did all the heavy lifting."

"Don't be silly. Here's to a job well done."

The two men clinked glasses, and Bill took his first sip.

Now, that's tasty.

"Hey! Where's mine?" said Frieda, from the other side of the counter.

Next to her, Rodney was helping himself to the charcuterie. A few feet away, Phyllis and Cindy broke off their conversation and stared at Bill. Cindy frowned, obviously displeased that he had served himself before the guests.

"Okay. Okay. Don't shoot the bartender. I have a fresh drink right here and another batch coming up."

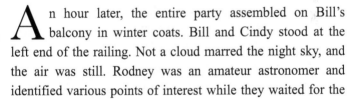

An hour later, the entire party assembled on Bill's balcony in winter coats. Bill and Cindy stood at the left end of the railing. Not a cloud marred the night sky, and the air was still. Rodney was an amateur astronomer and identified various points of interest while they waited for the show to begin.

The promotional efforts for the show had borne fruit, and groups of people gathered on nearly every condo balcony on the ridge. More people stood on the ground below, bundled in coats and sipping from travel cups. Bill hadn't seen Wintergreen this crowded since Independence Day.

Bill heard the drones long before he saw them, an eerie sound of a hundred flying machines humming in unison. And then, all at once, a blue wave formed in the hollow, rose to a high crest, and crashed toward the Mountain Inn. A chorus of wonder rose from the audience. In an instant, all lights disappeared, only to reappear shortly in the form of a massive white ball hovering high above the ski slopes. Slowly, the ball grew smaller and turned orange, and then a purple ring formed around it. The ring spun in a slow circle around the orange planet. Spectators clapped and shouted their approval.

The drones continued to awe the crowd with their magic. A giant snowboarder performed tricks. An avalanche of snow crashed down the mountain, and then an enormous blue buck with antlers charged back up the hill. The show climaxed with an imitation of fireworks. A roman candle showered the sky with sparkles of red, white, and blue that then reformed into a giant flag of stars and stripes.

Then, darkness. Gradually, the humming dimmed and then stopped altogether. The crowd chattered with excitement on the balconies and the hillside. Bill's guests took turns sharing their impressions of the show. Silently, Bill was thankful that technology capable of rendering death could also bring happiness to the world.

Cindy moved to stand behind Bill and wrapped her arms around his middle. He caressed her hands. They were leaving in the morning for ten days in Florida. They would spend a few days at the theme parks and then a week in Melbourne. Swimming, reading, restaurants, and long walks on the beach.

Bill and Cindy had discussed their relationship at length and reached what he considered a satisfactory though imperfect arrangement. For the time being, they were together, an item, a pair, a couple understood to be with one another and not with anyone else. As for the long term, no commitments. This was a non-negotiable term from Cindy's perspective. Bill had learned through their conversations that Cindy remained shaken by her divorce. For many years, she had believed her marriage would last until death, and when it didn't, she lost all respect for the concept of ever-after love. So be it. Bill remained delighted with her company and found her terms preferable to the alternative.

Cindy brought her cheek next to his and said, "It will still be cold when we get back. Very cold."

Bill pulled her arms more tightly around him. "Sounds comfy. It's a perfect time for building fires in the fireplace."

"And what about in the daytime? What will you do then?"

"I'll be busy with a new project."

"Yeah? What's that?"

"I'm getting a dog."

THE END

~

Thank you for reading *Murder in White.* I hope you enjoyed Bill O'Shea's latest adventure.

If you haven't read books one and two, now is a great time to read the full series.

The Mountain View Murder (Book One)

Retired homicide detective Bill O'Shea moves to the Blue Ridge Mountains to enjoy a peaceful retirement. Then the community police ask him to help investigate an accidental death. Will Bill solve the case, or will a Wintergreen murderer go free?

The Overlook Murder (Book Two)

When an aging entrepreneur falls to his death, the local police ask Bill to help with the investigation. Forensic evidence soon convinces Bill that the death was no accident, and there are more than a few suspects. Will Bill and his friends solve the crime, or will a Wintergreen murderer go free?

Both books are available now in ebook and print versions on Amazon and in the ebook version at all major online stores.

Join the Readers Club to make sure you don't miss the next Bill O'Shea adventure. As a bonus for signing up, you'll get a free Bill O'Shea story.

The Curse of Crabtree Falls

When a friend invites Bill to hike Crabtree Falls, he eagerly accepts, but then he hears the story of the curse. Not given to superstition, Bill is compelled to investigate the mysterious waterfall that has doomed lovers since 1851.

www.patrickkellystories.com/newsletter-signup

ABOUT WINTERGREEN

Several years ago, we bought a condo in Wintergreen, Virginia, to escape the hot Texas summers. Not by coincidence, our condo is in the same location as the one owned by Bill O'Shea. Groundhogs scrounge greens from the lawn beneath our balcony. Sadly, the groundhog named Mr. Chips is a fictional character. Black bear sightings and stories are common.

As portrayed in the novel, Wintergreen has an official policy against flying personal drones, but I have heard stories of rogue drone sightings.

Most of the places and establishments mentioned in the story are real; however, the characters and events are all fictitious. The Wintergreen Police and Fire & Rescue teams do a fabulous job of protecting the community. The police and rescue procedures depicted in the novel are from my imagination and undoubtedly an inaccurate portrayal of how real first responders go about their business. As a writer, my interest lies primarily with the mystery and the interaction of the characters.

As always, my wife Susie tried to help me write a better book. She is the love of my life.

ACKNOWLEDGMENTS

Sleepy Fox Studios designed the book cover. Liz Perry of Per Se Editing edited the manuscript.

Several Wintergreen residents were kind enough to read an early draft and give me feedback, including Emily Ferguson, Valerie Calhoun, Terri Ann Brooks, Linda Ehinger, and Debby Missal.

A special thanks to Fire & Rescue Chief Curtis Sheets, who generously shared some tips on how mountain search rescues are conducted. Despite his best efforts, my depiction of the search for a missing hiker undoubtedly includes innaccuracies. I am entirely to blame for those errors.

Thank you to the many people who work hard to make Wintergreen a wonderful resort community.

Praise for *The Wintergreen Mystery Series*

"The prose was compulsively readable, well-written, and engrossing. The pace was steady and character-driven. There were plenty of suspects and the ending was unexpected with a nice twist." **- PamG, top 100 Goodreads reviewer**

"The Mountain View Murder" is an excellent start to a new mystery series. Protagonist Bill is an instantly likeable main character, and I enjoyed learning more about him as the story progressed." **- Barnes & Noble reviewer**

"I found this book intriguing, suspenseful, full of twists and turns. I found the storyline riveting from the first word until the last word." **- Barnes & Noble reviewer**

FIVE STAR AMAZON REVIEWS!!!

"The spectacular descriptions of the Appalachian mountains, and true to life engaging characters make this a book to come back to. I'm ready for the next in the series."

"Wonderful characters are woven into a suspenseful whodunnit that will make you laugh and cry. Welcome to The Wintergreen Mystery Series. It's going to be a fun ride!"

KEEP IN TOUCH

If you enjoyed meeting Bill O'Shea and his friends at Wintergreen, lend me your email address, and I'll keep you posted on their next adventure.

www.patrickkellystories.com/newsletter-signup

Follow me on:

www.goodreads.com/patrickkelly

Instagram: pkellystories

Facebook: patrickkellywriter

Made in the USA
Las Vegas, NV
02 October 2023

78474690R00159